OCTOBER RITES

Andrea and Brenda, clad only in bras and panties, positioned themselves on either side of the billiard table, near Buddy's head. Nick, holding the knife and book, climbed up onto the foot of the table and knelt, moving forward on his knees until he rode Buddy's midsection. He straightened his back, his head nearly touching the Tiffany fixture that hung from the ceiling.

"Sorry, Scalizi," he said, "but someone has to be sacrificed."

"What are you doing!" Buddy screamed. He yanked desperately at his bonds, tried to raise his hands off the table.

"Say the words," Nick said, handing the book to Andrea.

Andrea found a marked spot in the paperback. "Saman, great Lord of the Dead, take this offering. For in you, death is life."

Backman brought the carving knife high until it bumped the lamp. Light rocked nightmarishly across Buddy's eyes. He saw Nick Backman lower the knife toward his heart—

"No!" Buddy screamed. . . .

OCTOBER

AL SARRANTONIO

BANTAM BOOKS
New York • Toronto • London • Sydney • Auckland

OCTOBER
A Bantam Book/ October 1990

ISBN 0-553-28630-7

Published simultaneously in the United States and Canada

Bantam Books are published by Bantam Books, a division of Bantam Doubleday Dell Publishing Group, Inc. Its trademark, consisting of the words "Bantam Books" and the portrayal of a rooster, is Registered in the U.S. Patent and Trademark Office and in other countries. Marca Registrada. Bantam Books, 666 Fifth Avenue, New York, New York 10103.

PRINTED IN THE UNITED STATES OF AMERICA

RAD   0   9   8   7   6   5   4   3   2   1

FOR CHARLIE GRANT,
THE FATHER OF US ALL

JOHN OF LOURDES: Was there another place to
    go?
    Was there another season
    At the end of days,
    That led, finally, to
    Winter?

THE PROPHET: Yes. And already
    You know its name.

> —EDWARD, LORD OF YORKE
> *The Prophet of Time*

There are men from cold Northern Lands
And one, from farthest South
Equal parts Snake, and Worm, and Lizard,
Who is their Lord, and dwells within them, and,
When he is wont, makes them die.

> —SEBASTIAN CAPLET
> *The Lord of Death*

And then they made fire to him,
And prayed,
And sought to ward him off
For one year more.

> —ROBERT HAMBLING
> *The Druids*

BOOK ONE

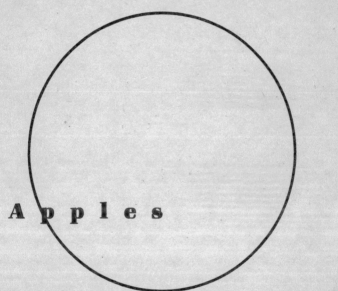

Apples

1
October 1st

*There was a time when all the world was green and cold,
when all men were as one man, and the days echoed, mountain through valley to mountain, with October smell. There
was a time, one beautiful morning, when all the world
smelled of apples.*

James Weston reached his hand up, admiring the gold
sheen of the hairs on his arm, the sharp red line of plaid
where his checkered shirt cuffed wrist, the long curve of his
fingers, the dirt beneath his fingernails. He reached his hand
up slowly, imagining himself in a movie, not the one he had
been in but the one he played in his mind to amuse himself.

His mind was often, to him, a better place than the
world. In his mind, the world could be green and cold whenever he wanted. Mountain could call to mountain, apples

could bloom, pink-white petals to hard ripe fruit, whenever he wished.

In the movie of his mind, he froze the hand, admiring the warm new sun on it, the morning cold; and then he began to move again and the hand touched and then grasped the apple it had reached for and then froze.

Admire the apple, he thought in his mind's sound track. *Feel the taut skin stretched tight as a woman's abdomen over child. It holds similar fruit; the fruit is burst leaf to flower. Remember the flower.*

His index finger moved up to stem, traced the line of stem to branch.

Umbilical. Life cord.

He tugged at the apple. He felt the reluctance in the stem, the resistance to letting go.

Choice, his sound track told him, the cameras of his eyes locked in stasis on the reluctant apple. He felt his hand on it, pulling, gently insistent, felt the tree, roots, trunk, branch, pulling in reaction against him.

My choice, he thought.

His fingers tightened on the apple, began to twist.

Mine.

His fingers opened, letting the apple go.

He watched the apple pull back up into the tree; the sigh of leaf against leaf in his head sound track became a joyful whisper.

He laughed, swept his hand down in a long arc to the ground, to snatch a fallen apple. The tree's willing gift. His hand lifted to his mouth, the apple finding purchase between his teeth, good crisp juice squirting down his tongue into his throat.

He took the apple from his mouth, laughed again, chewed his earned bite with relish.

The dog at his feet looked up at him expectantly.

"That's the way the world's supposed to work, Rusty,"

James Weston said, laugh half-leaving his mouth with his words, eyes darkening around the corners where thoughts were left to the emotions of the face.

He put his hand into the long shag coat of the dog, rubbing deep, drawing solace, pleasure from the act.

"That's the way," he repeated, almost inaudibly. His mind movie stared off over the dog and the valley of apple trees between two mountains, to a place where movies stopped and the world really was.

He was a tall man, and lanky. Those who gave him a first look and little more often compared him to Abraham Lincoln. He had, in fact, played Lincoln in the movies not three months before. They had lengthened his forehead by waxing and removing a half inch of his front hairline; had thinned his hair, straightened the thick curls that tended to congregate to either side of his part; had changed the part from right to left. They had built his nose, made it longer, fleshier; deepened his eyes for effect—though his eyes, hooded and gray, already nearly matched Lincoln's own. He had learned to change his smile, from the slow thing that tended to blossom to full-blown grin, to a melancholy line that merely lengthened and creviced with dark humor. He had accentuated his stoop; had learned to hold his hands behind his back with solemn sadness. He had learned to weep without shedding tears; had learned to throw his leg over the arm of a chair when sitting in it, not so much sitting as hanging upon it, all angles, as a crane might look if forced to sit on furniture. He had learned to nod slowly, and speak thoughtfully and resonantly, though Lincoln's own voice was high and did not carry. He had learned to do all these things, and he had played through the Civil War, watched it unfold for him as it had unfolded for Lincoln, and Lincoln had slowly seeped into him, taking over his bones.

On the last day of shooting, after his last scene, a wooing of Mary Todd shot out of sequence—having already watched, in other scenes, her dissolution—he quietly took off and folded Lincoln's coat, and placed it on a chair, black stovepipe atop the pile, walked from his trailer, and kept walking.

He had been wearing then the same clothes he wore today, white stiff shirt, long pants and suspenders, and black shoes with thick soles, and the steps of six months had worn the soles down, and led him from Abraham Lincoln to here —to, he hoped, himself again.

He felt the regular, quick bellows of the dog's huffing under his hand. The dog, a red setter with eyes that looked as though they held laughter, met his gaze and barked hoarsely, then continued to huff, tongue lolling.

"What is it, Rusty?" he said, lowering himself to the ground, crossing his legs to meet the dog on his own level. "You hungry?"

The dog huffed again, without enthusiasm. Around them were scattered the cores of half a dozen apples, equal dinner for himself and Rusty.

"What is it then? Thirsty? Want to run?"

In answer, Rusty lowered himself to the ground, paws before him sphinxlike, head resting on one forearm.

"Tired?"

Rusty shifted his head to his other forearm.

Weston put his hand on the dog's head, rubbing deep. A sound not unlike that of a cat's purr issued from Rusty's throat and he closed his eyes.

"Let me think," Weston said. He studied the apple trees, spaced in files around him, studied past them the darkening autumn blue sky, the hard-edged cumulus clouds lazily sailing southeast. For a moment his thoughts slipped to metaphor: he thought himself a ship sailing southeast with the clouds, with sails full unfurled, heading from Vancouver, foreign port, mock America for a mock Civil War, to New York, home port—where life waited for him to begin again.

He focused away from metaphor and saw the sky again; the clouds had moved beyond the trees and were gone, leaving him behind. Only clear, night-deepening blue remained, ocean or sky. Cold nevertheless. Maybe that part of his life, and the pain that waited for his living it again, could wait.

Maybe he wasn't ready for that pain yet, again.

His eyes shifted from sky to trees overhead.

Maybe he could work, pick apples.

He laughed and stood up. "All right, Rusty." The dog watched him contentedly as he stretched up, shouting at the protestation of his tired bones. It was early autumn, early in his life. They would sleep in the midst of apples. Tomorrow, like today, the chill would leave the world for a while as the sun played weakly at Indian summer. He would roll up his sleeves and stay in this orchard and pick fruit.

"It's settled, we'll stay," he said to the dog.

Unthinking, forgetful of the inner movie he had so recently reviewed, he ignored the fallen bounty around him, stretched his hand out to a nearby tree, and twisted an apple from its stem, with a viciousness that would have frightened him had he known it was there.

2

October 1st

Where is Lydia? Teatime has passed, it's growing dark. You'd think she was still a child, so forgetful.

Such a cold fall day, I can feel it through the window glass. The trees shorn of foliage, the apple orchards look like winter—

What is that feeling? A chill on my fingertips, running through my hand like electricity to my elbow, I know that feeling . . .

The Time Machine.

I laugh, pulled suddenly from the present, in the void between memories, between tired, broken axons, not knowing where I am or where I will land.

Don't the metaphors ever stop?

It's like this, some days. I laugh again, on the cusp between years. Alzheimer's disease. Presenile dementia. I know all about it, in the flashing moments such as this, when I belong to nowhere, anchored in it firmly. I know the Time Machine my mind has become.

I laugh once more.

No, the metaphors never stop.

I feel content in these brief instants of clarity between present and past. Disembodied, but still myself. Not part of the continuum of physics, the meat-and-potatoes world. Mind. The Time Machine is my ill mind.

If only I could control it. If only I could stay here, in this dreamworld of disembodiment.

But always I land, the disease a firm hand on the controls (there, another metaphor!), and even now I feel it pressing so insistently against my spine, against the soft, lost sponge of my brain, guiding me to a landing.

The Time Machine . . .

Oh! Oh! The sky is falling!

I laugh, thinking about Chicken Little, and Danny thinks I have forgiven him and puts his hand on me, but I push him away. Cold, the first chill morning of autumn, heat ticking through the radiators, frost covering the grass when I looked out the kitchen window and there he was coming home, the bastard. He entered through the back door smiling, sheepish, unrepentant, little huffs of breath steaming from the outside cold, all those toys in his arms for Lydia and the boys, that big Irish grin and everyone melted, *I* melted for a little while, and the children playing in the parlor with their presents while he ran his big hands over me in our locked bedroom and we were wed once more.

He puts his hand on me and I push him away again.

"What's wrong?" he asks, and I try to rake his eyes out, but he holds my arms and hits me in the face once with the flat of his hand and laughs again. I tell him I will leave and he almost hits me again, but instead he laughs. "Remember Rhea?" he says. That was 1940, only ten years ago, and

things haven't changed. Her husband, Brant, beat her, she
tried to kill him but he beat her even worse, and the cops
laughed about it and drove away. They called her Wildcat. I
saw from the curb as I walked home from school. Her lip
cut down one corner, two eyes black like a raccoon, I think
he broke her nose but they didn't set it because he wouldn't
bring her to the hospital, they had no money except for his
beer. After the police left I watched the door close and
heard him beat her some more. That's what happens when
girls try to leave, the unwritten code of men. I felt sorry for
her, but like everybody else I avoided her after that. When
you try and fail, you're a failure. It was as if she had a
disease. Wildcat, they called her, bad wife.

So the children play and Danny laughs. But it is an un-
easy laugh. To see me mad again he lies back and smokes a
cigarette, looking at the ceiling with a wistful look on his
face. Then he turns toward me, bedsprings creaking under
him, and says quietly, but not gently, "It's not as if I love
'em, Eileen." He rolls back, staring at the ceiling, smiling.
"You can always write about it," he adds. He concentrates
on his cigarette, waiting for me to scream and beat at him or
leave the room, so I leave, and I hear him just laugh once, a
snort, and I wish I could hate him more (bad wife) but I
know this is his only weapon against me, against memory . . .

The Time Machine, back to the present . . .

It's so dark now, the cold through the window, that horrible cold in my hand, my arm . . .

Time . . .

Eddie, stop eating like that!

Pawing the food into his mouth as if he has two stom-
achs, ignoring me, just like his father. And he the youngest.
He even laughs like Danny. I thought Bobby would be like
Danny, the influence of proximity, but he's quiet and reads
all the time. In my secret heart, where I keep my dreams,

Bobby is my hope just as Lydia is my little girl and Eddie is lost to me. I dream for Bobby. Danny calls him names, when he's deep in his six-pack, yells at him for not going out for sports like his brother. Bobby answers by getting sullen. I fear for him because there's fire beneath his brooding.

One day I tried to talk to him but he would not confide in me. It would be nice to have someone confide in me. Mary Wayne used to confide in me—

"I just like to be alone," he said.

My heart was bursting with hope for him, for myself. "I found some of the things you wrote."

His face reddened in embarrassment and anger. It was as if I had asked him about wet-dream stains on his sheets.

"It's only that—" I began, wanting to tell him how beautiful his thoughts are, that he should continue to express himself. But these words would not come out, only my fears. "I'm afraid you'll run away."

His face was still flushed with anger. "Anything to get out of here."

I didn't know what to say. A gulf between us, one I didn't know how to bridge. I realized that Bobby was lost to me, too. All children are lost to their parents. We never possess them—only cradle them until they learn to cradle themselves. From birth they are their own.

"Never let guilt, or fear, rule you," I said to him, thinking of his father. I left him to his brooding, and I'm afraid, lying here next to Danny and his beery snores, that Bobby will indeed run away . . .

Time . . .

That freeze in my arm—I've felt it before . . .

Again, to the past . . .

Oh! The sky is falling! Bright red and gold! Chicken Little, just like they told us in grade school . . .

Yes, Mother, I said, I lost my reader, please don't hit me, it was an accident. Please—

But of course she hit me, and here I am with the sun going down, the sky cooling, and she's airing the quilts out on the line. They blow, giant autumn leaves, that's a metaphor. Mrs. Greene would approve. And, like Chicken Little, I say the sky is falling, which is something like a metaphor, red and gold and shades-of-brown leaves, dropping pieces of the sky. The sun makes patches of deep gold light on the spaces between the trees. It shines like a gold beam on the carpet of falling sky. Oh! The sky is falling! And it feels so good to dance away from the window, my pigtails flying out, I see them from the corners of my eyes, I feel like I'm in the sky, falling with the leaves, falling!—

Yes, Mother, I'm sorry I was making noise. No, I mean yes, I would like some supper. I'm sorry, I didn't think before I spoke. Please, Mother, I promise next time—

"Damn you," I whisper fiercely as the door closes, but she doesn't hear and I clamp my hands over my mouth to keep from saying more. I'm sorry, God, for saying such a thing to my mother, but she hasn't been kind to me lately and I don't think it's all my fault. She thinks I don't know she wasn't married to my father, but I know. I found one of the letters he sends her with money. Columbus, Ohio. He must be a good man to do that. I may run away to him if she doesn't let me go to the party next week. I hear Mr. Fields out there now, in the parlor. I'll ask her when he leaves.

Would that be a bad thing, God? To run away? I wonder if you can hear me up there. Above the falling sky.

The sun is almost gone. Squinting, I see sparkles of it low through the oaks. The dropping leaves break up the sparkles and give them different colors. Mrs. Greene said I am good at reading, have a good imagination, but that my penmanship should be improved if I want to be a writer. I told her I would buy a typewriter. I think she thought it was funny, though she continued to look at me sternly. She doesn't think I'm silly, I hope. I do want to be a writer, unless I fall in love and marry a prince, and live in a castle. If that happens, I'll have supper whenever I like . . .

The Machine once more, pulling me back to now . . .

Lydia, is that you? Why don't you come? My arm, it feels frozen, as if it's made of cracking ice . . .

And pushing me back, firmly, to then . . .

No, I didn't mean to be sharp with you, Mother. Yes, I forgot to get the bread and the milk as you asked, but that's only because I'm so *excited.* You *did* say I could go—but you did! Last week, when Mr. Fields was here—

Damn you! Damn you!

I'm sure she heard me, but all she did was slam the door harder. *Damn* her. I'll run away to Columbus, to Father. He would let me go to parties. A banker, written on his bank stationery. I wonder what she does with the money. Assistant manager. I wonder what Columbus is like.

The trees look like skeletons, shorn of acorns. The squirrels have squirreled them away. *Apt,* Mrs. Greene would say. I'll run away, be a writer, in my room with a typewriter in Father's house. It would be a big house. A banker. I'll be like Emily Dickinson. Is Columbus like Amherst?

Tree skeletons, flecks of red and gold skin shed around them. A broken carpet of flesh. Creepy. So is Jerry Martin, of course, but—

Damn her! Everyone will be at that party, and they'll know I'm the wallflower they think I am. Eileen the Meek. When all I am is a tragic princess, trapped in a movie. Cary Grant will stroll in, smiling, and save me. "*Darling,* how simply dreadful for you to be in this con*di*tion." Dancing, dinner, banter, a kiss under moonlight—

Halloween moon. I bet they're all getting their costumes on now. I wonder if Mother even lit the candle in our pumpkin, the one *I* bought, damn—

Mother? I didn't hear you come in. Yes, I'm sorry I used

that word. Yes, I asked His forgiveness. I'm sorry, God, heartily sorry—

I can go? Oh, Mother, thank you! Yes, I'll get dressed now. Thank you! Thank you!

Of course I hear Mr. Fields cough out in the parlor and that's why she wants me out of here. But who cares! Thank you, Mr. Fields! with your bad breath and dry, nervous hands. He looks like a bird on a perch. I throw on my costume and walk out past the parlor. He looks at me with those tiny eyes of his behind his steel-rimmed glasses as I go by. He gives me the willies, but I almost laugh, I have to put my hand to my mouth because I'm dressed like a black cat and he looks so much like a bird. I hear him cough again as the storm door closes behind me, and then I do laugh out loud.

Then, I'm running down the steps, into the night—

I can't believe I'm going to this party!

And such a beautiful night! How to describe this night? Mrs. Greene would like this: stars white as cold milk against raven-black sky, trees like skeletons (that's still the best!), leafless oak and birch branches rattling like bones in the wind. Leaves, fallen, the colors of a red rainbow, fighting each other, twirling, crackling down the gutters, snapping at the roots of trees they've left, as if trying to decide whether or not to jump back on.

Too *flowery,* of course. But Mrs. Greene would love it. And I love this night! Pumpkin flames snapping in the breeze, children flying from door to door like wind-borne wraiths.

Suddenly I'm running, wind-borne, too, a black cat with wings! Pumpkin eyes wink as I fly past.

I can't wait to get to this party!

And—there it is!

The party house!

A strange house. How to describe it for Mrs. Greene?

Too grim for metaphor: what's a metaphor for darkness? No pumpkin, no light on the porch. Too dark even to be haunted. It looks like an inside-out house, wearing its soul on its gutters and shingles. Metaphor, after all: the porch running the length of the house a mouth with missing railing posts for gap-teeth, the door in its center a gullet; slate-blank windows for eyes; at either end of the top floor, jutting above the roof, peaked gables are horns.

Wary of going in, I hide behind a hedge. I watch as someone dressed like a witch (Marsha Denby? How appropriate!) runs up the tongue of the walk, skips up the steps onto the porch-mouth, jumps into the esophagus.

I can almost hear the house belch as Marsha disappears into darkness.

I don't want to be swallowed by this house.

I don't want to go into that darkness.

But then here comes another one, in a miniature baseball uniform, number 3 on the back, fat like Babe Ruth, too. It must be Jackie Farmer, followed by a white-sheet ghost, twin spacemen (Bobby and Billy Seavers), a bat with flapping black wings. All are gulped down by the house. It belches muffled cheers and laughter discreetly through the front door.

Still I don't want to go in.

And then Mary Wayne appears and disappears into the house, and I *have* to go in.

Mary is dressed like a princess, of course: pink taffeta, jeweled crown, sparkling wand. I decide to call out from my hiding hedge, but she's up the steps and through the front entry before I can open my cat's mouth.

And then I'm running from my hedge, and over the lawn (the grass looks black, feels dead), up the porch steps (creaking like old bones, the wood rotted in spots). The door leans off its hinges—

I'm *in.*

I feel the house burp over my digestion.

Apt, Mrs. Greene?

It's so *dark.* Isn't there any light? Yes, ahead, an orange glow down the hallway. The floor creaks like the porch steps. The dry smell of dust. No furniture, until—*there,* a table covered with a sheet. I lift the sheet; under it—a milk carton.

Ahead, orange light strengthens. I hear laughter, still muffled.

A turn at the end of the hallway—and there's the jack-o'-lantern belonging on the front porch, set on another milk crate beside the cellar door. A very bad carving job, the eyes different sizes, barely triangular, large on the rind, chiseled down to tiny openings on the pulpy inside. The nose barely a slit, the mouth crooked, filled with peaked fangs.

A stifled cheer from the cellar. Someone says, "Of course, Mary . . ."

I take a step down the stairs, hesitate. Behind me, at the front of the house, two laughing voices. I know them. Danny Sullivan and Barry Meyer. I feel like a cornered feline. My heart is going too fast, thinking about Danny, what Mary and I have written in our diaries.

They're getting closer. Barry is making mock frightened noises. Danny tells him to be quiet. I step to the far side of the cellar door, backing away from pumpkin light. I watch them appear—Danny in football jersey and helmet, tall, Barry trailing bands of gauze bandage, a defective mummy.

"Wait," Barry says, holding Danny back from entering the cellar. I think for a moment I've been discovered; but Barry angles a small flask out from between two strips of white cloth enwrapping his jacket, opens it, tilts it into his mouth.

He hands it to Danny, who sips, making a face.

Barry snorts, "Come on, big shot, you told me you know

how to drink. From what I've heard about this party, you'll need it."

"What the hell are we doing here, then?" Danny asks sullenly, pushing the flask away. "Jerry Martin gives me the heebie-jeebies."

"We're here," Barry says, "because we told everybody we'd be here, and if we don't show up, it means we're chicken."

"The hell with 'em."

Barry puts the flask back up to his mouth, drinks. "What's wrong? Not *man* enough to face Jeepers Jerry?"

Danny gives Barry a sarcastic smile. "It was *you* who told me the guy was strange to begin with, after you tripped him up in the hall and he just stood there smiling at you."

I swear that Barry shivers. "Figment of your imagination, buddy."

"Then why are you drinking so much?"

"I like the taste of it," Barry says, slapping Danny on the back. "Don't worry, when you're a man like me, you'll get to like it, too."

They tramp down the stairs, Barry making Tarzan noises. I hear a grunt, the hingey creaking open of a heavy door. The noise level increases dramatically. Barry gives out a whoop and then the noise is suddenly cut as the door below is shut.

I step out of my hiding spot. I'm alone. I stare at the deformed visage of the ill-carved pumpkin and am seized by an urge to run like a real black cat, with real, not lipstick, whiskers, back into play-Halloween night, away from this real Halloween. I want to race until my cat legs tire, leap through the front door (no gullet) of my house, past startled, myopic Mr. Fields, past my mother, into my room, and crouching and shivering, hide under my bed.

I want to do that. I don't care what they think of me (chicken! not cat), I'm turning to go—

And then I hear someone banging through the front door.

I turn into the cellar doorway and step down.

Even dim pumpkin light deserts me. I put my hand-paw on the banister. It's covered with a sooty layer of dust. The wall is sheathed in dampness, like wet rock. The boards of the stairs shift as my foot touches them. I look back up at the top of the landing; a shadow fills the doorway, staring down at me—

Hurry.

The steps shift, I patter down.

At the bottom is a closed door. Light seeps from under it. I search for the knob. The wood on the door is clammy-cold. I find the knob and it turns, but the door won't give. I push against it with my body and it resists, then opens with a wet sound.

Sound.

Orange light.

I close the door as quietly as possible behind me. But someone has already spotted me. "Class treasurer!" Barry Meyer shouts from the back of the cellar. He grins at me. Danny stands next to him. I look away shyly but Danny isn't looking at me anyway. Mary Wayne has him by the arm. Danny has a green bottle of Coke in one hand but he's not drinking it. He has taken off his football helmet and is smiling at Mary.

Now that I've been announced, I'm invisible. No one has come through the cellar door after me. I remember that shadow staring down at me and shiver, moving deeper into the room.

Observe! Mrs. Greene would say.

It's almost as dark in here as upstairs. A flickering pumpkin in each corner set on a milk crate. The faces are no better on these than on the one upstairs.

A table is set against one wall, covered with a white tablecloth trimmed in orange and black crepe paper. On top of the table are Halloween paper plates, illustrated in broomed witches, scarecrows under harvest moons half-hidden in clouds. On the plates are iced cupcakes. White icing, an orange pumpkin centered in each. The pumpkins are ill decorated. Crooked mouth, small eyes. But the icing job is precise.

Barry's voice booms nearby. I turn to see him standing, back to me, laughing at a joke Ted Michaels, the class president, costumed like Gene Autry, is telling him. Barry's costume has unraveled even further; a nest of bandages trails behind him, threatening to tangle his shoes.

Suddenly Barry turns around and grins at me.

I begin to turn away as he says, his alcoholic breath now catching up to him, "Hi."

I nod, backing away, but he reaches out and gently takes my arm and says, "Can I talk with you?"

He is serious. *Blushing.* This is the same Barry I've seen stand in the middle of math class and drop his pants as Mr. Whitcover was busy at the blackboard with an equation; who stood up to the vice principal, daring to fight him after he'd been accused of stealing one of the small stone lions that guard the entrance to the school (he didn't; Peter Barnet did it, but Barry never told); who rigs water balloons in his locker, then pretends he's having trouble opening it so someone will help him, with predictably aqueous results. (I observe, Mrs. Greene!)

I look up at him; remarkably, his blush deepens. "Yes?" I manage to get out, still not trusting him. This could be one of his jokes, and considering his alcohol consumption, it could be a nasty one.

It is no joke.

A horrible thought strikes me. Perhaps when Barry's been with Danny, and seen the mooning looks I've tossed Danny's way, he has thought they were meant for him! (I can't help thinking of Scarlett O'Hara— "Why *Ashley,* you silly thing . . .")

"I, well, umm," he says, and then he's suddenly speechless.

So am I. My less-than-outgoing ways haven't loaded me with experience in dealing with boys. I have Mary Wayne's stories, which are mostly products of her fancy, and I have the movies ("Why, *Ashley . . ."),* but—*what am I going to do?*

"Are you all right, Barry?" I manage to croak out.

"Umm, sure," he says, and then abruptly he vanishes, turning tail, fleeing to the other end of the cellar. I blink my eyes. Now he's laughing and joking with Danny again, slipping his flask from his pocket and bringing it to his mouth.

I think perhaps I've imagined the whole episode, but he glances my way, flask to lips, and quickly looks away.

The door leading into the cellar makes a horrible creaking noise. I had forgotten the shaded figure at the top of the stairs. I shiver. I turn to see the door open.

It grinds ponderously to a halt, standing open. No figure has appeared. A cold chill has entered the cellar.

Bobby Seavers, who stands next to the open door, reaches to push it closed with his space-suited hand.

He shrinks back.

There *is* someone there. A black shape detaches itself from the surrounding darkness and enters the room.

But for the snapping of pumpkin candles, there is silence. The tall, wavering shadows of costumed guests thrown against the walls make the scene look like a fever dream.

The specter reaches a black-gloved hand to its shrouded head and freezes.

Everyone watches, mesmerized. Palpable fear grips the room.

The shrouded one screeches, a sound that penetrates to the high corners of the cellar. Billy Seavers jumps nearly a foot off the ground. I levitate at least eight inches. The spectre rips its coal-black shroud from its head, revealing—

Frankie Bargeti.

Billy Seavers reaches him first. I think he will beat Frankie's grinning face to unconsciousness, but others pull him away. Billy manages one punch, but that doesn't stop Frankie's laugh. His laughter continues even after he has been dragged to a corner and dumped on the cold floor. "Got 'em good," he squeals, holding his black-leotard-clad knees. His face, which resembles Charlie McCarthy's, spreads in a grin that threatens to split his cheeks.

The cliquish hum of the party gradually returns, punctuated by the high, annoying cackle of Frankie's self-congratulation. I may be the only one to see Jerry Martin, our host, enter the cellar.

He closes the door quietly and solidly behind him. He is dressed in the same kind of nondescript clothes he wears to school, dark green sweater, tan slacks, loafers. There is nothing about him save his difference to indicate that this is his party. That in itself I find unsettling.

He catches me observing him. Though there is absolutely nothing unusual about his noncommittal glance, I go cold inside. It is as if he had turned some chill, invisible ray on me. He makes his way unobtrusively to the back of the cellar and is lost to view.

"Well?"

Mary Wayne addresses me. She stands radiant, beautiful, a princess out of a fairy tale. I hate her. She makes me feel like Cinderella, with no ball to attend. This party is certainly no ball. My slippers are more patent leather than glass crystal.

"Hello, Mary."

"Wonderful party, don't you think?" she says airily. *"Danny* certainly thinks so."

I want to wipe the smug smile from her face, but restrain

myself. I comfort myself with the sudden, comical realization that she has patterned herself on Scarlett O'Hara. Oh, *Ashley!*

"He's *so* handsome," she continues. "I'll be going to the prom with him."

"He asked you?" I blurt out, comic realization forgotten, my own unrealistic dreams instantly dashed.

"You really *do* like him, don't you?" she replies cattily. "Ever since I told you the secrets of my heart, I've noticed you watching him."

I begin to tell her that it was I who first wrote of Danny in my own diary, long before she gave me her unwanted confidences, but she doesn't give me the chance.

"I feared something like this, Eileen Connel. Marsha Denby *told* me you couldn't be trusted. Well, let me tell you, he hasn't asked me to the prom *yet,* but he will, and I *warn* you to stay out of my way."

She turns and stalks away, a perfect Scarlett O'Hara in miniature. I don't know whether to laugh or cry because she is heading for Danny again, who stands watching a loud game of apple bobbing that has broken out in the middle of the room.

Everyone is drawn to this contest. As I join the circle of spectators, I discover why. Barry Meyer, of course, is involved, with Frank Bargeti. A big iron washtub is filled with water and round, red apples. Barry's and Frank's hands have been tied behind them with neckties, and they kneel over the tub, trying to snare apples with their teeth. There are six tooth-marked apples next to Barry already. There are none by Frankie, who has been picking up apples in his mouth, taking bites out of them and letting them drop back into the water, splashing Barry and everyone standing nearby. I overhear someone say that five dollars has been bet on the outcome; they will bob until the tub is empty. Five dollars is apparently a small price for Frankie to pay to be the center of attention, which he manages until Barry picks up an apple with his teeth to discover that Frankie has already taken a huge bite out of it.

Barry makes a stifled, disgusted sound. With the fruit still clamped in his teeth, he raises himself on his knees and releases the apple onto Frankie's head.

Frankie cries, "Owww!" and retaliates in kind.

Before long, amid laughter, the floor is soaked with water and broken apples.

"That's not the way the game is played," comes a cool voice through the laughter.

As if a switch had been thrown, silence descends.

Puffing, soaking wet, Frankie and Barry lift their heads from the tub and, resting back on their knees, regard Jerry Martin, who stands before them.

"Just a little fun," Barry says, laughing, still trying to catch his breath.

"Sure." Frankie laughs shortly.

"But it's my party," Jerry says. He speaks quietly, reasonably, but his words depart his mouth covered with frost.

"Yeah, well, listen," Barry says, grunting from his knees to a standing position. His voice is defiant, with the beginnings of anger, but then he catches my eye and the blush returns to his large, huffing face, silencing him.

Once again, the sound of snapping candles dominates the cellar.

"To heck with all this scaredy-cat stuff!" Frankie shouts abruptly. He has loosened his bonds and stands up, a full head shorter than Barry. He picks up an apple. "Join the party!" He giggles and darts forward, shoving the apple into Jerry Martin's mouth.

Time suspends for an instant. The apple stays in Jerry Martin's mouth, then falls to the floor, cracking open with the sound a beetle makes when you step on its shell.

Frankie stands still, his grin frozen to his face. "Gee," he says nervously, "just a joke."

Jerry Martin smiles, a thin, humorless gesture.

"Come on, a joke," Frankie persists. He titters. "Listen to this one," he begins, but then suddenly, Jerry Martin has pushed him down to his knees, face poised over the washtub.

Frankie's eyes widen as Jerry Martin forces his head under the water.

Everyone watches as Frankie struggles comically to pull his head from the water. No one laughs.

Barry says, "Hey, Jerry, enough, okay?"

Frankie continues to struggle, hands pushing at the lip of the tub, legs thrashing. It looks as though he really is having trouble. Barry pulls his hands from his bonds and kneels down beside. He tries to pull Jerry off Frankie, but cannot. Putting both hands in the water, he cradles Frankie's face, but still he is unable to remove him from the water.

"Somebody help me!" Barry shouts. Jerry Martin's face is calm as chiseled ice. Frankie's hands beat wildly at the sides of the tub. His body arches backward futilely. Barry, with Danny Sullivan and Ted Michaels, beat at Jerry Martin's arms, his shoulders, his head, but they are unable to make him let go.

I observe the drama at the washtub with horrified fascination, until my attention is drawn to a brightening in the orange glow that lights the cellar. The shadows are flickering with greater urgency. The white paper tablecloth, I discover, is on fire. Someone has deliberately opened the four ill-carved pumpkins, overturned them, and allowed their burning candles to drop, spreading fire from the four corners of the room. Tongues of pumpkin-colored flame, licking up across the Halloween crepe paper, are beginning to taste the ceiling rafters.

I begin to shout "Fire!" but someone beats me to it.

Jackie Farmer, in his Babe Ruth costume, says in a frightened voice, "Oh, God."

At the washtub, Frankie Bargeti is suddenly released by Jerry Martin. Frankie's body is limp as Barry pulls it back, mouth dripping breathed-in water, eyes bloated with suffocation.

Ted Michaels pulls at the cellar door, but it won't open. Fire has filled the room with bright light. I begin to feel small rushes of heat. The exposed beams overhead are crisscrossing with flames.

Barry pushes past the others to the cellar door. He gives it a mighty pull, but it doesn't move.

In the back of the cellar, Marsha Denby, in her witch's costume, screeches as a lash of fire whips down from above to ignite her black, peaked hat. Fire snakes hungrily down around her, enclosing her in flame.

I try to get to her, but a panel of fire drops down in front of me, pushing me back with its heat.

Barry leaves Ted Michaels and Danny yanking at the door and looks wildly around until he locates Jerry Martin, who is smiling benignly next to the dead body of Frankie Bargeti.

Barry stalks over to him and grabs him by the sweater. "Tell me how to get out!"

"No," Jerry says.

Barry wheels his fist back and hits Jerry in the face. Jerry falls and lies immobile, then sits up, holding a hand to his bloody nose.

A wall of flame roars through the room, dividing it. I hear Mary Wayne scream. The cellar has begun to fill with smoke. It is getting difficult to breathe.

Barry shouts, "Here!" somewhere nearby. He is standing on one of the milk crates, kicking off the remains of smoldering, upside-down pumpkin. Above is a small rectangular window. There is a latch on it that won't open. He reaches to pull off his shoe, but it is tangled in white gauze.

I take off one of my black pumps and hand it up to him. He smashes it through one of the black-painted window-panes.

A wave of cold air washes over me as the glass shatters. Barry breaks the other panel and pulls the rest of the tooth-like glass shards out of the frame.

The fresh air clears the smoke momentarily, revealing Danny tugging weakly at the cellar door, which is outlined in yellow fire. Ted Michaels and the others around him have collapsed; one boy, in a devil costume, rolls on the floor beating at the red, devilishly grinning, burning mask cover-ing his face.

"Danny!" I scream, but he doesn't hear me as the smoke closes in again.

"Come on, Eileen!" Barry shouts. His strong hands pull me up, push me through the window.

Cool night air assaults me. I lie helpless on the grass outside the cellar window, coughing smoke from my mouth, wiping it from my eyes.

Finally, gasping lungsful of air, I roll over and look back down into the cellar.

I hear screams. Cool air pushes smoke aside. I see Barry dragging an unconscious Ted Michaels toward the window. "Take him!" he shouts up at me, and I pull as Barry pushes. Soon Ted is laid out on the grass next to me. Barry disap-pears back into enfolding smoke, appearing a moment later with the limp form of Danny Sullivan.

As Barry prepares to lift Danny up to me, Jerry Martin appears. His face is sooted, his hair singed, his nose blood-ied. He smiles until he sees the open window, with me out-side.

"No!" he screams, his face becoming an unearthly mask of rage. "This is my night!"

Jerry rakes at Barry wildly with his fingers. He does not look human; in his keening whine, head thrown back savagely, mouth open round and wide, in his scrabbling grasp, there is something horribly inhuman, almost reptilian.

"Take him!" Barry shouts, lifting Danny toward me. There are long claws of blood on Barry's face and shoulders. Jerry continues to rake at him, trying to pull him down.

"Hold him!" Barry gasps, and as I pull Danny out onto the grass next to Ted Michaels, I look back to see Barry stumble.

I cry out and reach through the window and take hold of his hand. Jerry Martin, mounted on his back, reaches around to claw at his eyes. Barry screams. He lets go of my hand and collapses into the smoke and fire.

I hear horrible shrieks, followed by silence.

"Barry!" I call. "Barry!"

In the cellar there is only silence now, and the odor of burning flesh.

"Barry—"

Jerry Martin's face thrusts out of the smoke. He hisses out at me soundlessly. His features have melted away. His hair has burned to blackened scalp and skull, his eyes stare round and white from charred sockets, his mouth is fixed in a skull-smile.

His burned, bony hand grabs at me, taking hold of my wrist. I feel an icy, numb shock go through my arm. I twitch back, breaking contact, and he reaches out again, blackened bits of flesh falling from his hand, and misses me.

He breathes heavily, a ragged bellows. He struggles to maintain his position in the window. He slips back, claws with his bone-fingers, and pulls himself back up to the sill.

Then—

The Time Machine . . .

Oh, God, Lydia, is that you? A light goes on behind me; I hear the door open—God, please, Lydia, let it be you.

Yes, yes, I know I'm shouting. Didn't you hear me? I fell asleep in my chair. Didn't you hear me calling you?

Oh, God, why am I shaking, I can't stop shaking, my arm is so cold, so numb. I almost remember—

No, don't move me now, just let me sit here with my comforter, until I warm up. Yes, a cup of tea would be nice.

Come back quickly, Lydia!

What is that? Light in the yard! The porch light has gone on. Such beautiful colors, the leaves, falling leaves . . .

Oh! Oh! The sky is falling! No, that wasn't it, falling leaves, a terrible cold feeling. I know that feeling—

Halloween . . .

Oh, God, oh, dear God. Lydia, come quick! Oh, dear God, I can't stop shaking. I know that feeling.

Lydia!

Oh, dear God, I almost remember . . .

3
October 1st

For Kevin Michaels, there came a moment, somewhat past the beginning of the second movement of Johannes Brahms's Fourth Symphony, when the music blossomed to aching beauty.

As Kevin worked in the midst of open cartons of books in his new office, searching with growing frustration for an unfound pencil, turning over a legal pad where he was sure the pencil was hiding, the moment occurred.

The music had been on in the background, wafting from the small twin speakers of a portable cassette player mounted temporarily on the top shelf of what was, for now, an empty bookcase. For Kevin, the first movement of the Fourth Symphony was stately, slow in procession, marvelous—but easily relegated to the background when other, more pressing needs arose. He had put the cassette into the machine and forgotten it was on. But when the flowering of the second movement occurred, Kevin found himself standing perfectly still, the music commanding his ears, Svengali-like. The errant pencil was forgotten.

As so often happened at this point in Brahms's Fourth, tears welled in his eyes.

It occurred to him that, perhaps unconsciously, he had deliberately put this particular piece of music on.

I'm back, Father.

Tears pooled in the corners of his eyes; one spilled over to trace a wet line to his cheek and stop there, drying to salt.

Brahms knew all about autumn, about bittersweet feelings. Autumn was the bittersweet season, the beautiful, tender passing of the year from life toward death, from knowability to unknowability.

There was a stained-glass window, a thin rectangle of deep red, blue, and rose, set into the top of the wood-framed window in Kevin's office. As the moment of Brahmsian epiphany commenced, the sun, lowering through the tops of the oaks in the quadrangle outside, slanted its tiring rays through the stained glass and bathed the opposite wall in gothic light. The window was open at the bottom, chilling the room. Reluctant to close the window, enjoying the fall weather, Kevin had donned his gray, button, cardigan sweater, feeling more the assistant professor for it.

Now, a single leaf drifted down, spinning slowly like a dancer, oblating the colors of the stained-glass window before traversing the rest of the window. Pulled by the air at the open bottom, it spun into the room to balance on the edge of the sill.

The blossoming moment of Brahms's Fourth moved on to development. Another lone tear found its way from the corner of Kevin's eye to make a temporary tributary on his face.

I'm back.

He moved toward the window, edging past a teetering stack of book boxes that threatened to fall and block his way. Stained-glass-filtered sunlight blinded him momentarily as he passed through the angle of its rays. Then it was above him, once again flooding the far wall of the office.

He stopped at the sill. The leaf, a deep red with tiny patches of still-breathing green, fell from the sill and he caught it, cradling it in his hand. He found its stem with his fingers, turned it, brought it close to his eye. The leaf was moist.

Back.

Absently, he lowered the leaf to his side, caressed it while he looked across the quadrangle.

There was still green grass in the quad, to either side of the center walkway reserved for faculty and seniors. The grass would feel cold if he rolled in it now. He had often rolled in it in October and November, on campus as a young boy with his father. Proudly, he had walked that center boulevard with Theodore Michaels or, daringly, had run it alone when he thought that no one would see. Someone always did, of course, though nothing was ever said. The eyes from all the windows in all the offices and classrooms surrounding this central hub of the University of New Polk were naturally drawn here. The oaks were well tended, the lawns trimmed, the perimeter paths clean, always filled with activity. The energy of the college spilled into here.

And of course, this was where the pretty girls walked.

Kevin watched one go by now, lost in thought, head down, repeating something to herself out of a half-open book. He admired the relaxation of her body; tonight, after the exam she may have studied the entire previous night for, she might remove the ribbon that held her long hair back from her face, replace her glasses for contact lenses, her loose sweater with a much tighter one, and return to the self-consciousness of the social being. College students played, of necessity, two roles: one academic, one social—and still, after all this time, after his own undergraduate days here were far behind him, Kevin had to admit that he still much preferred the way this young coed looked now, in desperately quiet thought, to the way she would look later.

Which brought Lydia to mind—

There was a loud click that startled him. He turned. The Brahms cassette had ended; the tape machine had shut itself off with its characteristically loud sound.

Back.

It was chilly in the room now, and even with his sweater on, Kevin felt it. He notched the window down, leaving it open a crack. The sun, he noted, had lowered behind the trees, darkening the quadrangle; as he watched, a scatter of late-afternoon lights set high on the buildings turned themselves on. It was growing dark in his office, also; the stained-glass window glowed with feeble intensity against the far wall.

Off high to his left, he heard the *bong, bong* of the clocktower bell, set to ring at six o'clock.

At the last *bong,* someone knocked, a rapid tapping, the sound of a ring against wood, on his door.

"Come in," Kevin called. He turned from the window, stumbling into a stack of boxes as the door opened. Someone flipped on the light switch. A bank of harsh blue-white neons flooded the room.

"Not a very good beginning, Mr. Michaels," the sharp, thin, disapproving voice of Raymond Fillet, the head of the Literature Department, spoke from the doorway.

Kevin grinned sheepishly, straightened. "Hopefully, tomorrow will be better."

"Hopefully," Fillet said, unsmiling. In the same sharp tone, he added, "There's a small reception in Dr. Weiss's office in five minutes. Please be there."

Abruptly, Fillet closed the door.

Bastard.

Kevin righted the boxes. A spill of books had slid from the top of one open carton, and he picked them up. Hawthorne, Flannery O'Connor, Scott Fitzgerald—and Eileen Connel. He placed the others back in the carton, kept the Connel book in his hand. *Season of Witches.* It was her first book, and her masterpiece. For three months, he had fought to get this book on his syllabus. Sidney Weiss had finally sided with him, against Dr. Fillet, and the book had gone onto the list beside Hemingway, Faulkner, Salinger, and other Masters of Modern American Literature.

But now, Weiss was leaving for Northwestern University, and Fillet had been named head of the department.

Which meant, of course, that the battle wasn't over.

He placed *Season of Witches* back carefully in its box, left his office, and walked the short hallway distance to Sidney Weiss's office.

"All hail the young buck!" Henry Beardman said, raising his glass as Kevin entered. Beardman, a brilliant Shakespeare scholar who knew almost nothing else about literature, was already drunk. A pleasant, sad man when sober, he was an aging homosexual trapped in the mores of a time when the closet was an institution. That attitude, coupled with the curse of ugliness, which he held aloft like a banner, made him nearly intolerable when he drank, which was often. Weiss had told Kevin that in the past year, Beardman had begun to show up in class inebriated; and Kevin had chided himself on the evil thought, probably true, that the arc of Beardman's career and life had long ago been charted, and now, especially since the homophobe Fillet was about to wear the crown, Beardman would end in dismissal, and eventually, dissolution.

Kevin smiled politely at Beardman, moving past him to the back of the cramped office. It was neon bright in here, too, but here and there one of the long bulbs had flickered

out, never to be replaced. Long ago the college's mainte-
nance man had refused to come near Dr. Weiss's office, de-
claring it a hopeless firetrap and refusing to be the one to
start the fire. A snake of wires, leading to everything from a
copy machine to a coffeemaker, an electric pencil sharpener
and small television, was hidden somewhere beneath the oak
tables, sagging bookshelves, and behind the two desks, one
of which contained nothing but stacks of untouched student
papers, some of them dating back to 1960. Weiss had never
handed a graded paper back to a student, had always graded
verbally, and had never given anything below a B minus.
Raymond Fillet had once succeeded, after years of trying, in
getting John Groteman, the university president, to demand
to see one of those student papers. Fillet had maintained
that Weiss never even looked at them and gave out grades
indiscriminately—an outrageous charge, which, if true,
would have had dire consequences for Weiss's career.
Grotemen had finally relented. Weiss, sitting in his squeaky
swivel chair in the far corner of the room before his other,
workable desk, smoking a pipe, had smiled at Fillet and
said, "Pick a card, any card." Fillet had reached deep into
one back pile, produced a paper from 1971, and handed it
triumphantly to John Groteman, who opened the blue cover
to find a meticulously corrected discussion of Beowulf by a
student named Mason Johnston. Johnston had been back on
campus the previous October for a reunion; he was now
president of a small computer firm in Connecticut.
Groteman went through the paper page by page, noted the
grade of B plus on the last page, then handed it back to
Raymond Fillet.

"This is an excellent and sensitive correction job,"
Groteman had said, not hiding the testiness in his voice. "I
don't appreciate what you've done, Raymond. Put the paper
back where you found it, please."

While Fillet was blustering, fumbling to find the spot

from which he had drawn the term paper, Groteman had turned to Dr. Weiss and said, "Can I ask you a question, Sid?"

Weiss had smiled. "Anything."

"What are you keeping all these papers for?"

Weiss's smile had widened. "That's easy. When I retire, I'm taking them with me to read again. I've found there's more fresh thought in one student paper, borrowed and sloppy and rushed and half-reasoned and even erroneous though it might be, than in all the department staffs in all the universities in America."

Groteman had left laughing, Fillet trailing behind like an apologetic dog, and that had been the end of the term paper incident.

And here they were now, these same term papers, stacked even higher, waiting for packing and transport to Northwestern, where, no doubt, they would be stacked and forgotten once more.

Kevin moved past the desk to the cleared spot on the windowsill where two tall bottles of white wine stood. There were plastic cups nested between the bottles. Kevin poured himself a glass of wine and turned to see the foppish, myopic, disapproving figure of Charles Steadman, Raymond Fillet's graduate student protégé, regarding him with less than interest.

"May I pour you some wine, Charles?" Kevin offered diplomatically.

Steadman, who modeled himself on T. S. Eliot, down to a three-piece wool suit and watch chain, spectacles, and wry, practiced, composed countenance, glanced around Kevin at the bottles and made a sour face.

"Must they always buy wine by the jug?"

"It's more economical that way," Kevin offered.

"Yes," Steadman said flatly. His hand went to his waist, as if in pose, and he turned to regard Raymond Fillet.

Steadman turned back to Kevin with his expressionless face and flat stare. "I trust we'll be serving better from now on. Unless, of course, the ghost of Theodore Michaels dominates *that* department, also."

Before Kevin could react, Steadman walked away.

"All hail the departing hero!" Henry Beardman said, raising his glass as Sidney Weiss entered the room.

In toast, the others holding plastic cups raised them as Weiss blustered in, waving them aside. "Oh, *stop!*" he said. "I hate good-byes, and you all know that. So you have conspired to say good-bye in a grand way. You! Michaels!" he said, catching Kevin's eye. "Get me some wine!"

To Kevin's surprise, and momentary annoyance, Dr. Weiss waited at the doorway for him to bring the wine. When Kevin reached the door, Weiss took him by the arm and steered him out into the hall. "We have to talk."

They stopped a listening-ear's distance from the party, which continued. Sidney Weiss took the wine from Kevin and drank a finger of it. Then his eyes locked on Kevin's and stayed there.

"You're going to have trouble," Weiss said. "Fillet isn't even going to wait until I'm on the plane."

"But—"

"Please listen." Weiss's voice was stern, but Kevin detected a trace of smile. "This is what Raymond will do. He will try to invalidate your assistant professorship, claiming the appointment was made after I had decided to leave. Which is perfectly true. His contention is that I had no right to appoint you, that the decision should have waited until the new chair—himself, of course—was installed. His argument has weight—and unfortunately, precedent. A similar situation arose in the History Department a few years ago."

"What happened then?"

"The new boy was kicked out, and the new chair put in his own man."

"But—"

"Let me finish, Michaels! We both know Fillet wants Charles Steadman to fill your spot permanently. It's no secret. Another of Fillet's arguments is that it would be unfair to remove Steadman, who has merely been keeping your seat warm during this mess, at this point. If Steadman wasn't such an incompetent toady, I might even agree with that. But there are subtle politics at work here. I think you'll be all right if you do what I say."

"Which is?"

"Resign your position."

"What!"

Weiss laughed. "I'm glad your reactions aren't dulled by this lousy wine! You have to resign. In fact, we're going to march back into my office in two minutes and announce that unhappy event. Charles Steadman will continue teaching your class. Then, in a week or two, you will be reinstated, in plenty of time to finish your first semester."

Kevin looked perplexed.

"Let me explain," Weiss said. "When you resign, another, older precedent will take place. I found a case in 1958 where an identical situation arose. That time, the president of the university stepped in to make the appointment. That's what John Groteman is going to do now. When Groteman says something, it usually sticks like glue. The trustees rarely balk at anything he does, because he brings in money."

"Dr. Weiss, thank you."

"For what?" Weiss grinned. "This is what most of my job is, Kevin. I should warn you, though, that Fillet will be out for your blood."

"I can handle Fillet."

"I hope so. You know he's wanted this job of mine for a long time. He gave your father trouble twenty years ago, and he doesn't forget anything. You realize"—Weiss laughed—"you'll be number one on Fillet's list after this!"

"Quite a distinction."

Weiss laughed again, taking Kevin by the arm. "Come on, let's have some more bad white wine and watch the shock on their faces when we announce your decision. The way I figure it, this will give you extra time to get reacquainted with New Polk."

"I'd like that," Kevin said.

They began to walk, then Weiss squeezed Kevin's arm, making him stop.

"There's one thing I want to make sure you know before I leave," Weiss said seriously.

"What's that?"

"Your father's memory didn't get you this job, Kevin. Your talent did. The case you made for teaching Eileen Connel proved that to me."

"Thank you."

Weiss's hand continued to hold Kevin's arm. "I'm earnest about this. I don't want you to feel you have something to prove here at New Polk, that you have to clear your father's name. Ted Michaels was a great teacher before . . ." Weiss hesitated. "Before his trouble began. He helped me a lot when I was starting out. At one time, he was the best in his field. He was always haunted, but your mother was a wonderful calming influence on him. After he lost her, all that business from the past just took hold of him completely."

Weiss sighed, as if making a decision. "Look, you don't know this, but your father tried to have Eileen Connel's books added to the syllabus here in the late sixties. He failed, because by then his thinking just wasn't very clear.

"You've succeeded with that, Kevin, and you should consider it an honor to your father's memory. And frankly, I think you should let it stop there. I'm speaking as a friend, now. I'd hate to see you follow your father's path. I see the tendency there, and it bothers me. You're teaching Eileen Connel because she's a damned good novelist, not because she's privy to some secret knowledge denied the rest of us. You're going to have trouble enough keeping her books in the curriculum with Fillet fighting you."

Weiss's face softened. "I want you to promise that if it's ever too much, or that working under Raymond Fillet is unbearable, you'll call me at Northwestern. Will you do that?"

"I will."

"Good." Weiss laughed. "And would you tell me one thing? Why do you like Johannes Brahms so much? Why not Beethoven?"

Kevin smiled. "I read somewhere that Beethoven merely took on God, while Brahms took on something much harder, man."

"I like that," Weiss said. "He certainly would have had a tough time with a man like Fillet."

They began to walk, and as they came in sight of the office door, Weiss let Kevin's arm go and leaned close to his ear. "And keep an eye on Henry Beardman," he whispered, chuckling. "He may be an old souse—but he can still move pretty quick when he sees something he likes."

Later, after the party in Sidney Weiss's office had ended, the shock of Kevin's announcement superseding Weiss's departure and causing all of the bad wine to be consumed, Kevin stood alone in his darkened office. The weak yellow illumination of the quadrangle lights barely lit the stained-glass window, making the colors glow like ghosts. The room was chillier than when he had left it. In the near dark, he fumbled with the cassette machine, rewound the tape in it, began to replay the Fourth Symphony of Johannes Brahms.

He stood at the window. A lone female student—perhaps the same girl he had seen earlier in the evening—made her way across the quadrangle, using the senior walk. Her head was bowed against a cold breeze that had arisen. She held her books tight across her front, hugging herself. She looked cold. A few leaves pirouetted from the oaks, flashing bare red and brown in the lights before settling to the ground. The girl kicked at them unconsciously as she walked.

Kevin suddenly wanted to hold her, to warm her. To warm himself.

Up above, the sky was very black above the lights, very cold.

The second movement of the symphony began, proceeded on its stately course. Kevin's hands, on the sill of the open window, grew coldly numb.

The music reached the point of blossom, opened with aching, sad beauty. This was not false sentiment, but heartbreaking melancholy. Kevin felt an irredeemable sense of emptiness.

Who in hell am I?

Brahms knew autumn, knew of bittersweet inevitability.

Suddenly, Kevin was crying. His body hitched with sobs. He brought his cold hands to his face, covered his eyes. A pain filled him like that Brahms must have known; he felt helpless in this beautiful season.

I don't know who I am. None of us know who we are.

He saw his father, in the end broken by madness and stroke, lost, his skin translucent, yellow-gray, paper thin, his eyes pleading, unable even to lift his head from his pillow.

"Kevin," his father had said on the edge of that great darkness. He had gripped Kevin's wrist with fingers sharp and hard as knives. "She knows, Kevin. She knows but she wouldn't tell me." The grip tightened; he strained to lift his head, his eyes widening, staring at something approaching. "Ask her!"

And then he went over, and only the breath left him, an unanswered question frozen in his unseeing eyes.

Oh, Father.

Kevin saw Theodore Michaels as a young man, the great, wise eyes that even then had begun to fill with haunting. The strong hands held out to him. Kevin, five years old, broke into a smile, running from the doorway of his father's office where he had waited to be noticed, over the tassled, deep blue-and-red Persian rug, into the dim, dark-wooded, book-lined recesses of that sanctuary, into his father's arms.

"Kevin!" his father shouted happily, hoisting him up into his lap, smelling of pipe tobacco and gray wool, swiveling his chair back to the desk—that great expanse of leather-edged blotter, scattered papers, a globe of the world on its oak base, the looming gray typewriter. The large hands held him tight around the middle, hugging him.

"Can I use it now?" Kevin said eagerly, reaching out to the flat, round keys of the machine.

"Yes!" his father said, rolling a fresh white sheet of paper into the platen. "Type away!"

"And can I read all your books," Kevin asked, fingers poised over the keys, looking up into those eyes, that mirror of love, "and do everything you do? Can I know what you know?"

The briefest cloud passed across his father's face, then he smiled and said, "Of course!"

"Hurray!"

Then his father lifted him so gently, rose and set him down, giving Kevin the swivel chair.

And sometime later, when Kevin had finished his wild, incoherent lines of typing, he looked up to see his father standing at the window, hands behind his back, a tiny curl of new smoke hovering over the bowl of his pipe, staring out into the darkening world . . .

Oh God . . .

Kevin wept for himself, for his father, for his mother, whom he never knew, and for Lydia, and for the girl who had made her way across the quadrangle but would still suffer cold, wrapping herself with her books to fight it off, until she reached her room. He could not stop crying. Perhaps there would be no heat, and the blankets the girl covered herself with would not stem the cold that had climbed into her body. She would sit in the corner of her room on the floor alone, shivering, begging for help from someone who wouldn't listen. Perhaps the world would grow colder around her, cutting her off even more completely. The aloneness she felt would find equality in her chill, and would freeze her. She would cry ice, the tears of the dead. They would freeze to her cheeks, which had been beautiful, and which had been kissed by her own mother, and now were hard and smooth. Such was the whole world around her, each man in his corner shivering, waiting for ice, the inevitable, unstoppable end—

There was a loud click as the cassette player turned itself off.

Kevin took his hands from his face. He gulped in a deep breath of air, shivered, wiped tears from his eyes. The symphony had ended, meaning he had been standing here for perhaps a half hour—

One of us knows—

He shivered again, straightening his body. He wiped the remaining shimmer of tears from his eyes. He had not cried like that for a long time. He felt embarrassed, as if someone had seen him and disapproved.

Ask her.

He took a long breath and looked out through the window.

Yes.

I'm back, Eileen.

A leaf danced down outside the pane, mere inches away.

He looked down; it had landed on the sill. As before, the chill breath outside blew it in, threatened to topple it from its perch. Kevin reached and grabbed it. It felt wet and full. He lifted it to his eyes, turning his head slightly to use the outside light, and studied the leaf.

It was green and full and, up until a few moments ago, had been alive.

4
October 2nd

Sleeping.

He dreamed of apples. In his dream, a canopy of apple trees hung over him, a shroud of sweet, red fruit, bobbing, ripe, heavy spheres dancing to some hidden melody. Above, the sky was very black, but his orchard was suffused with light, as if the fruit itself glowed with fecundity, the trees, still green-leaved, healthy as madonnas.

He rose from where he lay and tried to reach one of the apples to eat, but the fruit was too far above him. He was very hungry. He wore his Lincoln costume, his tall hat and beard, and he found that when he tried to remove the beard it would not come off. The hat was stuck tight to his head.

Beneath the hat, he felt something move against his scalp, wet and uncomfortable. He struggled to remove the hat from his head. Above him, the apples danced to their own wind. He could almost hear their song: a high, thin keening like a choir of angels.

The thing beneath his hat became more insistent. He felt it curling around his scalp, trying to find entrance. He became desperate, pulling feverishly at the hat.

The apples continued to sway and dance and sing.

He screamed, and suddenly the hat came free. He threw it away from himself, shivering, and felt desperately around his head. His hair was gone; he felt only scalp.

The hat lay bottom side toward him. Something crawled from within it, a long, thin snake with legs, and as it left the hat, it broke into segments, and the segments went in groups to each tree and began to inch up them.

Desperate, he removed his heavy coat and struck at the snakelike creatures as they came from the hat. But he was unable to damage them. They continued their movement to the trees. He looked up to see creatures inch along the tree branches, out onto the farthest, thinnest limbs, and crawl down, one to each apple. The apples still swayed, and the singing continued, until the creatures began to bore their way into the fruit, with a faint rasping sound.

The apples jerked on their branches, and the angelic keening changed to a whispery scream. The apples turned black and began to fall from the trees. He screamed himself as the orchard shimmered away, and he was in a carnival in a wide cut field of corn at horrible night—

James Weston gasped and sat up. Disorientation assaulted him; for a moment he saw black sky and the bole of a nearby tree and felt something wet near his skin. Then the dream returned to mist in his head and the sky cleared to early morning, a purple-red dawn coming up in the east.

Rusty panted beside him, raising his head questioningly.

Weston sat still for a few moments, arms straight back, hands flat against the ground. He let the rising dawn, a beautiful shaded line of color, bleed the dream out of him.

His breathing steadied. He felt at his face; there was, to his relief, no beard, only a day's stubble to shave off. There was no hat on his head. His hair was in place.

"Okay, Rusty," he said. "Okay."

Above, through the spreading arms of an apple tree, he saw the stars of Orion fading into morning light.

The dog nuzzled at his arm, lay down, and put his head on his paw.

A tiredness still in him, Weston lay back on the dewed grass. Quickly, he sat up. There was still a chill in him. He raised himself up on his long legs and stretched. His up-raised hand brushed the hard skin of a ripe apple and he recoiled, then relaxed. He laughed nervously.

"Bad dream, Rusty," he said, perplexed at the continuing vividness of what he had experienced in sleep. Only now did he feel his feet back firmly on the earth, his mind back in this world.

Rusty huffed, looked up, rested his head once more.

Down the hillside, someone was approaching the sharp treeline of the orchard.

Weston stretched again, brushed himself off. Rusty sat on his haunches next to him, and James bent to pat the dog's head.

As the stranger broke through the line of trees before him, Rusty gave a huff.

The stranger came to an abrupt halt. "What the—"

"Sorry if we startled you," Weston said. "I'm afraid we spent the night in your orchard. I hope we weren't trespassing."

The stranger came closer. Weston could make out a red plaid jacket, a weathered face under a beaten tweed cap, tan pants, heavy boots.

"Actually," the stranger said gruffly, "you *were* trespassing." He eyes Weston solemnly. "Eat any apples?"

"Yes . . ."

The stranger turned his gaze on Rusty. "That dog eat any apples?"

"Yes, he did."

The stranger cleared his throat, spit to one side. "I guess you like apples, then." He stepped closer, held a hand out. "I'm Ben Meyer. You've been eating Meyer apples, the best goddamn apples in the Hudson Valley."

Weston smiled, took Meyer's hand, shook it. "I'm James Weston, and this is Rusty."

"Glad to meet you, Rusty," Meyer said. "You, too, Weston. You hungry for something other than apples?"

"Why, yes—"

"Then help me out up here, and we'll go down and get some breakfast."

Without another word, Meyer tramped past them into the forest of trees.

Following solemnly behind, James and Rusty watched Ben Meyer stop at each block of trees, reach up, yank one apple from its stem, taste it, throw it aside. He moved deftly, stepping around occasional stones and once over a stone fence into another section of the orchard.

In twenty minutes they had covered the entire property. The sun had risen. The day would be cold and crisp. James noted that there were no clouds today coming from Vancouver; the air was clear and high.

"Romes need a little more time. Good day for Ida Reds," Meyer said finally, succinctly.

James and Rusty followed his brisk walk down the hillside, across a small front yard to a tidy farmhouse near a dirt road. The house had white siding and trim windows, a neat fence and tended garden. Nearby, autumned shade trees hung protectively over a lovers' swing. A stone walk curled up to the front porch. Next to the house stood a red barn.

"Martha! Guests!" Meyer called as they entered.

A small, tidy woman appeared in the kitchen doorway. She was neat as a porcelain doll, in her early seventies, aproned. A black terrier scooted past her and halted, its eyes going wide with surprise at the sight of Rusty. The terrier gave a high bark and chased Rusty back to the doorway, where the two dogs examined one another.

"Fast friends," Martha said, turning abruptly into the kitchen.

Ben led James into the kitchen. Meyer pulled off his plaid jacket, folded it over the back of a chair. He sat at the long kitchen table, pointed James to another setting his wife was making. Only when they were both seated with coffee before them did he turn his gaze to Weston again.

"So, you had yourself a sleep in my orchard last night. Mind if I guess the rest?"

James tasted the coffee, which was good, then smiled mildly. "Sure."

"Let's see." Meyer scratched at his chin, which had not been shaved. "You didn't come from New York City. That's for sure. Would have chased you straight off if you had. Don't like that place. But maybe you live in a big city."

Weston smiled. "So far, so good."

"I can't quite figure your accent. Mix of things. Good portion of upstate New York. California, maybe. I figure you live out there, now. Some other places, also. Maybe you traveled the country, picked some things up as you went."

Weston nodded, enjoying his coffee.

"And one other place, sort of like Canada, but not quite."

"Vancouver."

"Ah. Okay. Now your clothes, I can't figure. You didn't steal 'em, your frame's too tall and I didn't peg you for a thief. Except for apples, which is food to feed a belly. The clothes mystify me. That how they dress in Vancouver?"

"Not exactly—"

"Don't tell me, let me guess." He rubbed his chin, turned to his wife, who was opening eggs into a large skillet. "Martha, care to have a try?"

Martha turned around, leveled her gaze on James like a shotgun, and said, "He's an actor, Ben."

"Actor!" Meyer made a dismissive sound. "I never heard such foolishness—"

"She's right," Weston said.

"What!" Meyer turned with astonishment to his wife, who paused from scrambling the eggs in the skillet to give him a mild look. "It's no mystery, Ben. I saw him on TV."

"Well, I'll be damned," Ben said. Then suddenly Weston and Martha were laughing, and Ben joined in, too.

Their conversation halted while Martha served the eggs, with big slabs of Canadian bacon, slices of toast. She took off her apron and sat at her own place.

"You have to tell me how you guessed so much about me," James said.

"Tell him how, Ben," she said.

Ben waved his hand. "It's nothing. I traveled a lot, when I was younger. Army man for a while, then I sold things. Aircraft parts, oil-rig machinery, hydroelectric power plant fittings. When you spend a lot of time on the road, you listen to people. You observe. That's all there is to it." He turned to Martha. "And I observe this young man, who likes the way you cook, could use some more coffee."

With the mild knowingness that seemed to be her nature, Martha rose to fill James's coffee cup, as well as her own.

"When did you start growing apples?" Weston asked.

Ben smiled. "Oh, that would be . . ."

"Nineteen sixty-five," his wife said.

Ben nodded. "I was fifty years old that year. Tired of

being on the road. Martha here, she saved all the money, and I asked her what she wanted us to do. She said grow apples, like her daddy did. That was it."

"It's a good way to farm," Martha said. "My dad made a good living at it, and this town was a good place to do it." Her eyes seemed to drift away, to another place. Suddenly she fumbled with her coffee cup, got up, put her cup in the sink, and began to wash dishes.

Ben leaned over to whisper to James, "Don't mind her. It's just a way she gets."

Suddenly Martha turned off the sink tap and turned to level her gaze at James. The hurt, distracted look was gone from her face, replaced by puckish seriousness. "So tell us, Mr. Weston, is everything they say about you in those supermarket tabloids true?" Her mock frown deepened. "And just what are you doing on the road alone, in actor's clothes, with a stray dog that ain't your own?"

"Martha!" Ben scolded.

"I got an observer's eye of my own, Ben Meyer, and I notice things. Mr. Weston doesn't have to answer, if he doesn't want to."

James found himself smiling. "The two of you are like Sherlock Holmes. Rusty I picked up in Iowa. And no, almost none of the things you read in the supermarket are true. I just . . . had to get away. I was working on a picture, and the day it ended, I decided I had to be by myself for a while."

He thought that would satisfy them, but both Ben and Martha were eyeing him as if waiting for more.

"All right." James laughed. "I was seeing that soap opera star for a while, but that ended. She walked out on me, just like the newspapers said. But that's not why I left. Or at least not the whole reason. I was sick of California, sick of somebody doing everything for me. I was sick of being an actor, of pretending to be someone else all the time."

That satisfied Martha, who went back to her dishes.

"You have things to do?" Ben asked. "You'll be moving on?"

"Well . . ."

"You see, I was going to ask you to stay a little. It's time to pick Ida Reds, and I'm going to need help. That is, if you want to."

James now found genuine laughter welling up from inside. He threw his head back and let it out, and eventually the laughter subsided and he met the expectant gazes of Martha and Ben Meyer. Rusty had come to stand beside his chair, and James put his hand down to bury it in the thick coat of hair behind the dog's ears. He looked down to see the same expectant look in the dog's eyes; the black terrier had already curled up beside Rusty, appeared to be contentedly asleep.

"Want to stay, Rusty?" James asked.

The dog huffed in answer.

"If you hadn't asked me," James said to Ben Meyer, laughing, "I would have asked you."

5
October 7th

Sometimes, Davey Putnam wished he was back in grammar school. Things were simple, then. You worried about going to the dentist, you worried about getting a shot at the doctor's, you worried about nothing else. Dad went to work, Mom cleaned the house, you watched TV when you came home from school, and you did your homework at six o'clock. Sometimes you played touch football in the street until it began to get dark and the streetlights buzzed on in the autumn cold, or on Friday afternoons, you went looking for Indian arrowheads. On Saturday, you raked leaves in the morning, smelled them burn in steel-webbed trash cans in the afternoon. Sometimes you and your friends raked the crisp leaves into a huge mountain and rode your bikes at top speed into them. On Sunday, you went to church in the morning and read the funnies when you got home, ate

Mom's bacon, and crumb buns from the bakery, and watched cartoons on television. Sometimes Dad had a catch with you in the backyard, throwing perfect spirals with the football until it was time for the Giants game to come on TV. Sometimes you watched it with him, or went down into the cellar to run the HO train set on the board he had helped you build, or your friend Bobby Doyle came over and you went through your comics collection, or argued that football cards would never be better than baseball cards. In two days the World Series would start, and the Yankees would win again, and Reggie Jackson would hit a bunch of home runs. In a couple of weeks your biggest worry would be what to wear on Halloween, and what kind of bag to keep your candy in.

And then, overnight, they tried to make you grow up.

Oh, the world had been like that, then. That had been the real world, then. But then another real world had come and knocked on the door with a big fist, and the dentist, or a shot on the butt with a doctor's needle, had not been big worries anymore, only baby fears that were put to sleep with all the other baby toys, like Sunday afternoons and your mother's rotten meat loaf, which you hated but which sometimes made you cry now, when you thought about it, because you really did love it after all because it was hers. The big fist of the other, second real world was a simple thing, as simple as a small woman in a big car who didn't watch where she was going and rammed headfirst into your father's two-year-old Buick, throwing your mother in the passenger seat through the windshield, turning her into a vegetable in a dirty white room somewhere for a few months before death came, and killing your father outright. The little old lady walked away from the accident and said she was sorry, she made just too wide a turn in that Cadillac, she really never drove that often.

You were eleven when the second real world came knocking. And your uncle Rich up in Buffalo couldn't really take you in, he wasn't married and they had always said he was funny anyway, and bingo, there weren't any other relatives. So, at the age of eleven, the foster homes started, and the nightmares that became the real world, replacing the old one.

The old real world was like a receding dream, something Davey had once had and that the Big Fist had pushed away, and he watched it push farther and farther back into his memory, like something he had seen once on TV, maybe after school, a funny cartoon, and could barely remember.

He twisted the cap off another bottle of beer, stowing the empty he had just finished carefully in the bottom of the paper bag between his knees. Oh, they would kill him all right if they found out he was drinking beer. How they would disapprove. And the social worker never even looked in the refrigerator where the smiling asshole, good old Jack Carpenter, had twelve cold ones stowed away, plenty of empty cases out in the garage, if the girl with the sweater and the new college degree had bothered to go out there and look, or bothered to ask him anything at all instead of avoiding his eyes. So ole Jack merely waited for the idiot from social services to leave, then started in on his wife. The punching bag, ole Jack liked to call her. Tiny as a mouse, with the big eyes. Meek as a stuffed animal, until Davey had found she had climbed into his bed with him one night, after ole Jack had passed himself out, and was doing things to his privates even he hadn't thought of. The Mouth, Davey had called her after that, sometimes to her face.

Davey took a long swallow from the beer and stretched his blue-jeaned legs down the porch steps. The backyard was dirty. That was another thing they never looked at. Ole Jack cleaned it when he knew they were coming, but usually it was tobacco road, bald tires leaning like drunks against the paint-peeled garage, empty cat-food cans on the shadow side of the porch, crabgrass a half foot high between the dirt patches. The neighbors had tried to have them kicked out once, an ordinance for them to clean up. Ole Jack had cleaned up. They told him they would take the boy away, a sixteen-year-old shouldn't live in this kind of environment, but no one bothered to tell social services, and when the new idiot came the next week, another sweatered, flat-chested, earnest girl with photocopied forms, everything was fine. And then she went away, and the crabgrass grew back up, and they fed the cat on the back porch and let the cans fall off, and the front of the house was just as unmowed, and ole Jack never took the garbage cans in from the curb.

The beer was gone. Davey reached into the bag for another. "Shit," he said. The bag was all empties, but then he found a single cold bottle sitting among the warm empties and pulled it out. He twisted the cap off, tossed it at the bag and missed; a cursory search did not turn it up.

"Screw it," he said, turning the cold bottle up to his lips.

"Davey boy, what you say?"

For a moment Davey froze, the bottle to his mouth, thinking it was ole Jack home early from work. But his blood began to run again, and he turned to see Buddy Scalizi, the gate open behind him, entering the yard.

"Close the gate," Davey said.

"Sure." Scalizi smiled. He retraced his steps, using his bopping gait, head moving up and down as if he were snapping his finger to some beatnik beat in 1959. He was short, disheveled, thin black wisp of a beard tracing his chin around his lip. He wore a stained denim jacket. His eyes were a striking blue, and his teeth, when he smiled, were almost pure white, standing out.

"What's shaking, Davey?" Scalizi had closed the gate, was looking at Davey's beer bag with interest.

"Sorry, last one," Davey said with only a trace of apology. He finished it down before Scalizi could inevitably ask to have it.

"Shit," Buddy said. "Got any money?"

"Broke as your old man's car," Davey said.

Buddy laughed. "You can bet on that. What you been up to?"

Davey shrugged, dropped the empty bottle into the bag. He carefully rolled it closed at the top, readying it for disposal.

"Bet your old man'd whack you good, he caught you drinking." Scalizi made a face. "Especially that Genesee ale."

Davey made a slight smile. "What's going on, Buddy?"

Scalizi shuffled his feet. "Not much. You been to school?"

"Screw school," Davey replied.

"They're talking about sending Johnston around for you again. I was in detention yesterday, heard in Dean Whitiker's office—"

"Screw Whitiker, too. And Johnston. I'm not going back."

Scalizi shook his head. "Wish I had your balls, Davey."

"I bet you do." Davey grunted sarcastically. "Rubbed your own just about off."

Scalizi paused between laughter and anger, until Davey abruptly laughed.

"Jeez, Davey, sometimes I don't know whether you mean things or not."

"I never mean things, Buddy." He looked away, out over the backyard. "It's all bullshit."

"Well . . ."

Davey turned his eyes on Scalizi. "You gonna tell me why you came?"

"Yeah, sure—"

"Is it Backman, again? College boy been bugging you?"

"Sort of. Say's I'm a chickenshit."

"You are." But then that thin smile again, and Buddy smiled, too.

"Want me to kick his ass for you?" Davey asked.

"If you got nothing else to do."

Davey stood, moved the muscles in his shoulder under his jacket. He picked up the rolled bag of empty Genesee bottles in one hand, abruptly reached out to punch Scalizi lightly on the shoulder.

"Shit, no, I've got nothing else to do."

New Polk was an easy town to walk, a neat square bordered by main roads, surrounded by flat farms and apple orchards, rising up quietly from the Hudson Valley. Davey and Buddy walked the neighborhood, through the park with its shedding autumn trees, kids on playground rides, a few sweatered college kids with their girlfriends, high school boys playing touch football or grouped together to talk about girls or tomorrow's big game. The high schoolers moved aside when Buddy and Davey came near; when Davey deliberately veered close, they moved even farther away, with desultory glances, trying to look as if they had been thinking of moving anyway. Davey recognized his childhood friend Bobby Doyle among them. Davey walked with a practiced strut, a James Dean affectation that, with his open leather jacket and white T-shirt, his tight jeans and boots, made him look as fearsome as he wished. He had worked at his bad reputation, and people stayed out of his way. Scalizi followed behind with his bopping walk, looking like a puppy following his master.

Through the park and out the other side, past the sloping green of the University of New Polk to the left, the leafy, shaded, now-denuding oaks of the more affluent section of town on the right. They strode into this neighborhood, parting its waters like the Red Sea. There were nurses with baby carriages, BMWs and Jaguars parked at the curbs, sleek black driveways leading to white New England clapboards and the occasional contemporary with cedar siding and domed glass skylights set like monstrous portholes in the roofs. The lawns were tended, still green, the inevitable rock gardens trimmed, bright with late annuals. Davey kept his eyes averted, passing one particular house, white with deep-green shutters that had once been red, the house of his other, first real world. . . .

They turned right, passed similar scenery, turned left on another corner.

A black-and-white police cruiser appeared ahead. "Uh-oh," Scalizi said.

Davey said, "I see it."

They slowed their walk, banished the strutting. The patrol car approached, angled toward them, stopped to let them catch up.

The window on the driver's side rolled down, and the hard-lined, crew-cut, unsmiling face of a uniformed police officer regarded them. "Out for a stroll, Putnam?" he said humorlessly.

"Yes, Officer Johnston, I am," Davey said, forcing irony into his politeness.

"I thought I told you not to stroll here," Johnston said. "Especially not with Scalizi."

"I'm sorry, Officer. I guess I didn't hear you."

"Get your hearing checked. What are you doing here?"

"We're on our way to Nick Backman's house to get help on some of Buddy's homework."

"What about *your* homework, Putnam?"

Davey said nothing.

"Get what you need and get the hell home." The officer turned back to his steering wheel, revved his engine. "I'll be around to talk to your old man."

The officer let the patrol car begin to roll, then braked it. He turned to glare at Davey. "You hear me?"

"Yes, Officer," Davey said.

"Any trouble, it's your ass I haul in, whether it was you or not." This time he hit the accelerator.

"What is it with that bastard?" Buddy said. "Why is he always on your tail?"

Davey watched the patrol car turn the corner. "He had some trouble with my old man once." Before Scalizi could say anything, he added, "My *real* father."

Nick Backman's house was a block ahead, painted the inevitable white with black shingles. The driveway, which sloped slightly down to a garage set into the foundation, was empty.

"Let's go around back," Buddy said, resuming his strut.

They walked the flagstone path to the left of the driveway. There was a green chain-link fence at the backyard, tripped with a latch. They opened it and entered. The backyard had just been mowed, wheel marks of the mower in fresh ranks. The pool, near the back right corner of the yard, was covered with a tied green tarp, flecked with blown leaves and grass.

They went to the sliding glass door off the porch. It was locked, covered on the inside by a curtain. The windows along the back of the house were curtained.

"Dragged me over here for nothing," Davey said. "There's nobody home."

"He said he'd be here," Buddy protested.

"Well—"

A glare of light caught Davey's eye. There was a light in one of the basement windows set down into the foundation. As he watched, the light was eclipsed.

"Somebody's in the cellar," Davey said.

They went to the window. It was long and narrow, double paned, screened.

"See anything?" Buddy said.

"Be quiet."

Davey got down on his knees, brought his face close to the window. Buddy crouched beside him.

The light was once again blocked. As Davey watched, the figure blocking it stepped back. A long, white, naked body was revealed, ample breasts with standing nipples, long dark hair, the tight roundness of buttocks. Someone stepped forward, another naked female, to cup the left breast in her hand, guide it to her mouth while the girl with the long hair threw her head back, closed her eyes, opened her mouth—

"Jesus, that's Andrea Carlson," Scalizi said. "And Brenda—"

"Hello, boys."

Davey and Buddy pushed themselves up from the window to see Nick Backman, hands in pockets, regarding them mildly from the edge of the porch. The sliding glass door was open behind him, the curtain billowing out. Backman wore a deep-gray crew-neck sweater over the collared, buttoned wings of a blue oxford-cloth shirt. His creased gabardine slacks were cuffed, bottomed by oxblood loafers.

"We—" Buddy began.

"No problem. Come on in."

Backman turned, climbed through the sliding door.

"Jesus," Buddy said. "I can't believe—"

Davey took him by the arm and said, "Let's go."

They followed Nick Backman into the house. The sliding glass door led into a playroom, large-screen television centering one wall, a couch, a couple of easy chairs, a leather recliner angled around a coffee table covered with copies of *Vogue* and *Architectural Digest* along with the current *TV Guide*. The room was dimly lit. Nick Backman stood between the kitchen and playroom, near an open doorway with a downward staircase, waiting for them.

"Close the door, please," he said, and Buddy turned to slide the heavy glass frame closed.

"Lock it," Backman added.

After a moment's search, Buddy located the flip-switch and secured the door.

Davey balled his fists, stood facing Nick Backman. "You think because you're a couple of years older you can fuck with Buddy? I told you last year in high school to leave him alone. I don't give a damn if you're a big man in college now. The same—"

"Forget that," Nicky said, smiling. He turned to Buddy, and now Davey noticed the glassiness in Backman's eyes. "I'm sorry about that business. It won't happen again."

"Well . . . okay," Buddy said defiantly. "But if it does—"

Backman's smile widened. "It *won't*." He faced Davey. "I want to show you guys something."

Nick turned and descended the cellar stairs.

"This is weird," Buddy said. "I swear, Nick is high. That was Andrea Carlson down there. And Brenda Valachio."

"Want to check it out?" Davey asked.

"If you want to. But I swear, Nick was high. Did you see—"

"He was," Davey said.

They descended the stairs into a well-paneled cellar, neons set into a dropped ceiling, wall-to-wall carpeting, sailing-ship prints in double-matted frames on the walls, furniture that might once have been in the playroom upstairs, a frayed couch against the stairwell wall, two slipcovered chairs huddling nearby. A billiard table squatted under a long Tiffany-style hanging lamp. Along the far wall, under the row of windows giving view to the backyard, was a long bar, curved edge at the right end, a real barroom rack behind it, filled with spout-topped bottles of scotch and liqueurs. Over it was a mirror etched with the Budweiser eagle, topped by a clock.

On a wall mount at the end of the bar was another television.

To the right, abutting the bar was a paneled wall with two doors, one of them ajar.

Andrea Carlson and Brenda Valachio rose from the couch. They were dressed, New Polk preppie, sweaters, gray and blue, circled at the neck with pink flowers, white shirts, short button-collared beneath, washed jeans, white socks, penny loafers.

"Hi, fellas." Andrea Carlson smiled. Brenda's smile quickly widened and she bent over, covering her mouth, tittering.

"Hi," Buddy said. He flashed his white teeth, embarrassed.

Andrea Carlson held Davey's even look for a moment, then turned to take Brenda by the arm and say, "Stop that!" before beginning to laugh herself. Davey noticed a glassy look in Andrea's eyes.

"Where's Nick?" Buddy said.

"He's—" Brenda Valachio began, pointing toward the doorway by the bar, before collapsing into giggles again.

"In here, fellas!" Nick called. He appeared, motioning them to follow him into the room. The girls went ahead, holding each other, laughing.

Buddy leaned over, whispered to Davey, "This is fucked up."

Davey paused at the doorway. It was almost dark within, musty smelling. He saw something flickering in a far corner. The light of a single basement window from the front of the house threw bare illumination. In the shadows, he saw the outline of an overhead bulb, unpulled, saw the boxy shape of what looked like an oil burner.

"Come on in!" Nick called.

Davey went in; Buddy followed.

Davey's eyes adjusted. A tool bench sat against the far, unpainted cement wall, tools on Peg-Board above it, sloppily kept. No dropped ceiling. Bare support beams. Off to the left, canned goods on a bank of pine shelving; to the right, the oil burner; behind it, the source of the flickering light.

Andrea's head suddenly appeared, looking around the oil burner at them. "Come on!" she said impatiently.

"It's cold in here," Buddy complained.

As they approached the oil burner, they heard a mewling sound. There was the flicker of a candle flame. Reflected in it was the curved side of a coffee can resting on the cement floor. Andrea bent over it, reading something from a paperback book.

"Davey, I don't—" Buddy began.

"Quiet."

They moved around the oil burner into a cleared-out area. Boxes had been pushed aside; the disassembled skeleton of an old bed was jammed against the wall, nicked pine boards up under the rafters. Dust balls slept in the corners.

The area in the center was cleared.

A single candle, waxed onto a saucer; next to it, the empty blue coffee can; out of the can butted a wooden utensil handle.

The oil burner suddenly flared.

Davey felt Buddy jump beside him.

"What the fu—"

Nick, his back to them, turned. Something struggled in his hands, cupped at his middle; a small thing, brown, a tiny leg pushing out, trying to free itself from Backman's grip.

"Whoa, there," Nick said, laughing, holding the thing up. He pushed his thumbs under its ears to make them stand out, its little legs dangling, running in air. A cocker spaniel.

"Cute puppy, heh?" Nick said.

"Let's do it, Nick," Andrea said impatiently. She threw the book down. On the cover were three witches, putting things into a caldron.

"Okay," Nick said. "You ready, Davey? We needed five to make the coven complete."

On the cellar floor, Brenda was sketching a pentagram, a five-pointed star, with a piece of chalk.

"I don't think—" Davey said.

But in a blur of motion, Nick Backman forced the puppy to the floor, pinned it on its belly as Andrea drew the wooden handle from the coffee can, revealing a steak knife tapering to a bright point. She jabbed the knife forward, blocking the dog from Davey's sight.

"Do it!" Brenda said.

There was a yelp and an explosion of red. Nick yelled, bringing his hands up. A wash of liquid rose from the cellar floor, bathing all of them.

Davey stumbled back. Buddy said, "Shit!" throwing his hands to his face and then gasping. Frantically, he wiped his hands at his eyes.

"Oh, my God," Buddy cried. "Oh, my God."

"All *right!*" Nick cried. He lifted up a small, bloody mass, suspending it above the candle.

"And now—" he began solemnly, before blurting out a laugh.

Andrea and Brenda dissolved into giggling as Nick dropped the red thing onto the floor.

"Oh, *Jesus,* you should have *seen* your *faces!*" Backman screamed, pointing at Davey and Buddy. "You should have *seen—*"

Nick collapsed into laughter, holding his middle. The puppy, safe and whole, scooted out to sniff at the red, pulpy thing on the floor and then yelped and ran off to another part of the cellar.

"Catsup and water!" Brenda laughed, tears filling her

eyes. She reached down to squeeze the red-soaked sponge on the floor. "It was catsup and water!"

"I can't *stand* it!" Andrea howled, turning away from them, rolling on the floor.

Davey advanced on Nicky. Once again his fists were balled. "You bastard—"

"No—" Nicky said, still laughing. "It was . . . just a joke. Just a joke." He picked up the paperback book. "We got it all from this. I've got to read it for a frosh English class at the university." He kept laughing. "Give me your clothes, I'll wash them in the machine. You can have a little snort whle they're cleaning. I've got some coke somewhere . . ." He broke off in laughter. "The stains will come out. We've done it before." He looked at Andrea and Brenda. "Haven't we done it before? Taken off our clothes?"

The three of them exploded in laughter.

Davey clamped his hand on Nick's shoulder. "I'll break your goddamn head."

Nicky's face sobered. "No, you won't." He looked at Andrea and Brenda, who were still howling, and gasped a laugh before looking evenly at Davey. "You won't do anything, because I'll call the fucking police if you do and report you broke and entered my parents' house. Maybe you used to be a big shot when your old man was mayor, but your old man's long dead and now you're just a delinquent punk. And Scalizi is a coward who needs a punk to do his fighting for him." He looked down at Davey's hand until Davey removed it from his shoulder. "Leave."

Davey turned, walked out of the cellar.

"You gonna let him get away with that, Davey?" Buddy whined. "You gonna let him treat you like that?"

"Yeah, you gonna do that?" Backman taunted.

Davey turned, walked back, threw a right at Nick's face, connecting on the cheek. Backman went down, landing on

Brenda Valachio, who said, "Hey!" and pushed Nick aside. Andrea continued to laugh.

"All *right,* Davey!" Buddy said. "You got him good."

Nick sat up, rubbed his cheek. "You're screwed, Putnam."

"Get him," Brenda urged, then laughed.

"Get him good," Andrea said. "Let's call the cops. Maybe we can wash *their* clothes."

Nick and Brenda broke into laughter. As Davey and Buddy left, Nick fumbled a small Baggie of white powder out of his pocket, letting the girls crawl their hands over him to try to get it.

"Jesus, Davey, I'm sorry I got you into this. You're in big trouble now," Buddy said. They left by the back door and made their way to the street.

It was getting dark. The streetlights were on, like sour lemon lamps lighting the falling leaves. Davey's beer buzz was gone. He turned up his collar, put his hands in his pockets; far off, he heard the tentative, dying wail of a police siren that abruptly died.

"Yeah," he said, "so what?"

6
October 10th

As Kevin feared, Lydia answered the door.

"Oh," she said, almost a tiny gasp.

"I should have called."

"No," Lydia said. She looked at her hands. "Actually, I thought you were Dr. Carpenter."

"I'm sorry."

She was still looking at her hands. "Come in."

She had not changed. She still wore the kind of clothes Kevin remembered as "Lydia clothes," white-laced necks, long skirts, heavy materials. She was a thin girl who covered herself from neck to foot, navy knee socks, black pumps. It was a uniform of sorts.

She walked quickly in front of him, leading into the sitting room. "Would you like tea?" It was early afternoon. Kevin had eaten lunch only an hour before.

"Yes, of course," he said.

The house hadn't changed, either. It never would. In Kevin's mind it was a shrine, a museum. It reeked of lemon polish, dark rubbed wood, Queen Anne furniture, amber illumination, coolness. He had come here often just for the atmosphere, as if willing himself into this world. It was just before Lydia's father had left that he had first come into the house; but even then, it was obviously a place that Eileen Connel had created, a place she owned, fostered, tended like a garden. The house itself was as much a creation of her mind as her writing.

Lydia, too, was as much a creation of her mother as the house; indeed, she was so much a product of her mother's dominating vision that she had remained, a fixture in a house apart from the world, when her two brothers were long gone. Her mother's domination had become as oxygen to Lydia; like a gnarled root, she had taken her place among the Victorian knickknacks, the ponderously tolling clocks with slow pendulums, the dark wood, the dusty confines of small rooms and dim, sour light.

"Do you still take sugar?" Lydia asked.

"Yes."

They passed through the narrow hallway, through the mahogany-framed doorway, into the sitting room. The polished ebony baby grand piano was there on the right. Its white teeth grinned at Kevin, yellowing Mozart sheet music propped on its brow. He danced his fingers over the high keys, let the tone of the piano make him remember this room, this sound.

"Do you still play?" he asked.

"Yes." Her pale eyes came up to meet his briefly; the brief, sad smile. "She likes to hear it in the evenings." A catch of laugh. "She knows the sound of the phonograph, I can't fool her."

"You're expecting the doctor?"

Again her eyes met his, pale, flat blue. Her gaze lingered, perhaps with the thought in front of her. *Mother.* "She . . . had a very bad night. Her mind . . ."

"May I see her?"

"I'll get tea."

Lydia left him to the room. The furniture, damask, photos in gilded frames on the tables, Lydia, Eddie, and Bobby, the father absent. There had never been domestication in the house, Kevin knew; only living, and waiting for Danny Sullivan to leave for good. Eileen Connel had not hid her rejection of her husband; it had bled, with a kind of surety Kevin longed to understand, into the corners of the foundation and turned in on itself.

In the end, Eileen Connel had not only forced Danny Sullivan out of her house but out of her life, renouncing his name.

Another picture, on the mantel over the fireplace. Lydia only, gazing into the camera lens with detached concentration. *It is time to take a picture,* someone, probably her mother, had told her. *Stand and have your picture taken.* And she had, as she did everything else in its appointed time.

"Have you thought of leaving?" Kevin had asked her soon after meeting her, when her bland despair had become evident to him.

"No," Lydia had answered; and though Kevin had laughed, thinking it appropriate, it had occurred to him that probably, up until then, she never had.

"I'm back," Lydia announced with a touch of brightness. She set the tray down on the wide coffee table. Smooth dark wood. Tea scent overwhelmed the tinge of lemon polish.

She sat beside Kevin on the damask sofa, poured tea, handed it to him. Her fingers, he remembered, smelled like lemon polish.

He took the tea from her. "Thank you."

"You're in New Polk to teach," she said matter-of-factly. She sat on the sofa so that she would not have to look into his eyes. "I read about it in the paper."

"Yes."

"You're going to teach Mother's work."

Kevin sipped tea, put the cup and saucer down. "Yes."

"I knew you would."

He didn't know what to say. He put his hand out for his teacup, felt her eyes on him. He turned, his mouth ready to speak, but no words formed. She was looking at him. The wan, blond, straight frame of her hair made her thin face, with her thin, long nose, the scatter of dry freckles like tears under the bridge, her paper-dry lips, the pale line of her chin, so close to the bone beneath, appear even thinner. Her fingers were long, slim. The nails were sensibly short, unpainted. When they played the piano, they struck the keys like twigs, did not caress them. Her music-making was sad but not accomplished—remote, perhaps meaningful to herself. He had always told himself that love for her had not grown in him because it was not meant to be. But it had been the image of her fingers on the white keys of the piano, playing Mozart or Brahms, the tiny pads of her fingers enrubbed with lemon polish, the brittle, lonely sounds that had come out, that had kept him from loving her. . . .

"I would have left with you that day," she said.

"I know," he said, and suddenly the memory of the day that was the crux of his relationship with Lydia, with her mother, when he had first come face-to-face with himself, came back to him as if he had been immersed whole in it.

He came a final time to research his Ph.D. thesis, to talk with Eileen Connel. She let him record her spoken words as notes. She did not like to talk about her work, but she had warmed to him, had opened a tiny lock to a tiny room out of all the large locks and rooms within her. His father had just died.

She was forty-six years old, then. She was often forgetful, the Alzheimer's disease, unrecognized, just beginning to inhabit her. She let him into her bedroom-study on the second floor, a final secret unfolded for him. It was a room much as he had imagined it; she had spoken of it often; and in his mind, he had been able to construct its dimensions. It was different from what he had imagined, but later, he made a note that perhaps this was her writer's mind at work again, her genius for metaphor. There was one large window with a tree nearby; swimming sunlight washed over the walls. It was a cold day outside, February, but the sky was bright, high, cold, and blue, like many February skies in New York.

She sat at her desk. The desk was populated with writing equipment. In the center an old Remington typewriter, almost laughable with age, but perfectly maintained. She had told him, elsewhere in his recorded notes, that there was a man in New Polk who had originally sold it to her and who repaired it when necessary. He cleaned it every two months. She had learned, after many years, to change the ribbons herself.

"I used to write on a legal pad, in longhand," she told him, opening their conversation by noting his inspection of the typewriter. "That was when my husband was still here. Even though I had saved the money for a typewriter, he wouldn't allow me to have one. So I wrote on ruled yellow legal paper. For a time, I even used a fountain pen." Eileen smiled, a small blossom, coming, perhaps, from that secret little room where he had hoped to break the lock. "Don't look so shocked, Kevin," she added. "I never used a quill pen, for God's sake, or had to dip into a bottle of ink."

She turned her chair partway toward him, splitting her attention between him and her desk. As always, she refused to acknowledge the running tape recorder that lay at Kevin's feet. The chair was straight backed, severe, with a doilied *blue pad on the seat. She wore a loose white sweater, what looked to be gardening pants—tan, large fitting—white socks, and loafers. So unlike Lydia. Her face was lined, full, the eyes tired, but when they concentrated on Kevin or on a question, filled with sharp focus. They were dark, slate-gray, speckled with green. When reading, she wore glasses, tortoiseshell, which magnified the tiredness in her eyes.*

"What else do you want to know about my habits, Kevin?" She smiled, and for a moment he thought she was mocking him, but was, he realized, mocking herself. The walls were lined with books, carefully tended, dusted, green, blue, brown spines. Keeping her thoughts, Kevin imagined, from the outside world. Over her desk was a small, narrow shelf, enameled white, supported by two cast-iron brackets sculpted in vines. The shelf held all six of her novels.

"How do you correct?" Kevin asked.

"With a pencil." She added almost petulantly, "I'm not a goddess."

"I'm sorry—"

She regarded him directly, and he felt now like a baby, uninitiated.

She said, quietly, turning in her chair to lean slightly toward him, both hands on her knees, "It's a mysterious process, Kevin. But it's not magic. It's a craft, like learning to carve, or make cabinets. When I started, I scribbled, like a toddler. The words, the tools, I fumbled them, didn't know how to hold them or point the blades. I got better as I worked. I wanted to work, which was the important thing. After a while, I found the handles of the tools, held them fast, made nice cuts with them." She leaned back, her hands moving with her up her thighs. "That's all there is to it." She stared at him for a moment, then put a hand to her forehead. "I think you'd better go, Kevin."

"Please—"

She seemed distracted. "I'm . . . sorry. I just think we should end this. I have nothing more to say to you."

A desperation, of which he was not even aware, rose in him.

"You have to—"

"No, Kevin."

"You have to tell me what you know!" The hand holding his microphone was shaking. He felt hysteria overtaking him, heard what sounded like another man's voice, frightened, obsessed, speak his words.

"Kevin—"

"You know! It's in your work, it overwhelms everyone around you, your children, it helped destroy your marriage— you know! It's like a secret knowledge, you're so sure of yourself, so strong—tell me!"

He stood up, clutching his hands like fists at his sides. He felt on the verge of tears.

Eileen Connel rose and came to him. "Kevin," she said. She put her arms around him, held him, put his head to her breast. Remarkably, he felt her trembling against him.

"Oh, Kevin," she said. "If there's a secret, I don't know what it is. Something happened to me when I was a little girl that changed me. You already know the story." She hesitated, took a deep breath. "But I don't remember what happened to me. I remember the fire, I remember being helped from the cellar, I remember Jerry Martin's face. But I don't remember anything else." Her grip on Kevin tightened. "I can't help what I am. Believe me, Kevin, I'm still human."

Kevin was still shaking. "But you know yourself! Tell me how you know!"

"It's in me," she said gently, "it's in my writing, but I don't know how. Please stop, Kevin. Look what it did to your father—"

A spell broke between them. Kevin, suddenly mortified,

drew away from Eileen Connel. Her touch lingered, and then she stepped back, closed her eyes.

"Go now, Kevin."

The tiredness had returned to her face, her voice. She turned toward her desk, picked up a paperweight, a blue flower with wide petals imprisoned in clear, hard glass. She was an unreadable monument to him, the curve of her neck, her hard profile.

"Yes." He reached to switch off his tape recorder.

He opened the door, his notes and tape recorder cradled awkwardly in his arms. When he looked back, Eileen Connel was facing away from him, head bowed, one arm draped over her typewriter. She let the paperweight drop. It hit the desk, fell to the floor, rounded side down. Kevin saw a tiny chip of glass reflect light as it broke off.

As Kevin closed the door, she whispered, "I wish I could tell you."

Lydia was waiting for him, sitting on the landing nearby. She stood, holding the wide, oiled banister for balance. She wore a robe, buttoned to her throat. Her feet were in thin, quilted, pink slippers.

Kevin walked toward her. Instead of letting him pass, she stood in his way. Her hand reached out, haltingly, to brush the hair away from his forehead.

"I don't—" he said.

"Come with me."

With his arms still cradling his notes, his tape recorder, Kevin followed her to her room. An oak door, large, which swung back easily on its hinges. Inside, her bed, a huge four-poster, a canopy on top, printed in dark flowers, long stems, thorns jutting beneath their petals. A comforter, red and white and dark green, was pulled back. The sheets were crisp white. There was wallpaper, pale vertical stripes, mustard yel-

low and cream, a small bookcase, a dollhouse on a low table by the window. White curtains, billowy. The day outside blue-white, cold.

She took the things from his arms, put them on a chair by the door. There was a long key in her side of the door. She turned it. There was a deep click. She removed the key, put it also on the chair. She turned, stared at him with earnest resolution.

Continuing to look at him, unsmiling, she removed her slippers. She carefully undid the buttons of her robe, beginning at the neck. The buttons were tiny pink shells. Her body, thin, pale, revealed itself to him. Her breasts were small, the isosceles patch of hair below her belly thin, pale blond. The curve of her thighs was slight.

She dropped the robe to the floor and approached him.

"I love you, Kevin."

She undressed him, moved him to the bed, brought him beneath the sheets. Her skin was like paper moving against him. Her eyes swam up over him, seemed to search him.

Her fingers stroked his face, long, thin, moving over him like brittle branches. He smelled lemon polish, wanted suddenly to vomit—

"Damn you!" she cried, pushing him away from her. She curled away from him, moving under the sheets to the far side. She hid her face in her pillow. Her hair was long, straw colored, like overripe corn. He saw the procession of knobs, her spine, down her back.

He held his tongue. She was weeping, her thin body shivering under the quilt. He left the bed and dressed.

"She can't take you from me!" she sobbed at him as he was turning the key in the door. He was cradling his things. He turned to look at her. She had pushed herself up in the bed. Her face was streaked with tears. She looked very small, like a little girl, hugging herself.

"I love you," *she said, and now she turned away from him, sobbing into her pillow.*

"I'm sorry," he said, and this time when he left, no one stopped him.

Lydia had finished her tea. The afternoon was darkening, mottled light through the windows dimming toward evening as the sun lowered. She held her saucer on her lap.

"I would still leave with you, Kevin," she said.

Holding her saucer, she seemed again to be hugging herself once more, distant.

"It's been six years," he said.

"Yes," she said.

"I don't know what to say."

"If you hadn't come here, I wouldn't have told you. When you were away, I wrote you letters, but I tore them up. They were foolish. When I opened the door, and saw you there, I . . . thought you had come for me."

He said nothing.

"You're the only one I've ever met strong enough to pull me away from her. You're the only one who's ever been around her that she didn't destroy, or absorb. That's why I love you. That's why she . . ."

Silence lengthened between them. Before he asked, she said, "Would you like to see her now?"

"Yes."

She put the teacup down, stood, brought him to the back bedroom.

It was dark, shadowed in the room. Lydia called out softly, "Mother?" and then turned the light switch on.

The room appeared empty. A made bed, white candlewick bedspread, two pillows. Flower prints hung on the walls. No books, no typewriter. There was a writing desk to the left of the door, two envelopes, a single pen. A footstool next to the bed, embroidered red and blue. A wing chair faced the window, away from them.

"Mother?" Lydia called, more forcefully.

A thin, veined hand appeared at the arm of the chair, waved feebly.

They approached the chair. Eileen Connel looked like a ghost. She inhabited the chair as if pressed into it, embroidered into the weave of its fabric. Her hair was pure white, thinning, uncombed. Her eyes had flattened to pale gray, the skin around them veined and weak. Her lips quivered, as if she were perpetually going to say something. The hand that rested on the arm of the chair looked like a dead thing, flat and wan; her other hand, in her lap, trembled spastically. She wore pajamas, a robe, open at the neck. There were white socks on her feet; a pair of blue slippers lay nearby.

"Mother, do you need anything?" Lydia said.

Eileen Connel turned her head toward her daughter. The eyes filled in a bit, the mouth quivered open.

"Get the shovel, Lydia," she said. The arm on the chair lifted, the hand clutched at Lydia's sleeve. "And the pails. You know Bobby and Eddie like the pails and shovels at the beach. How could you leave them in the car?"

She let go of Lydia's arm, pointed to the window. "Stop that, Eddie! Stop hitting that girl! That toy is hers, don't you have any sense at all? Where is your brother? Did he go with Lydia? I forgot to tell her to get the sandwiches. Are you hungry, Eddie? Thirsty?"

Her hand dropped to her lap. The face turned to Lydia, to Kevin. She studied Kevin. "Eddie?" she said.

"Sit there, Mother," Lydia said. "Sit and be quiet."

"You're not Eddie! Where is he! Why won't you tell me what they said!" The voice filled with indignation and fear. "Were you there with him? Did you see it? Damn you all, I don't care about any note! You police are all the same! You pry, and infer, but you never *look*! Did you see him do it with your own eyes? How do you know it wasn't murder?" She grabbed Kevin's hand, held it hard, a claw. Her face collapsed into grief. "Please, tell me it isn't true! Oh, please, not because of me. My Eddie wouldn't do that to himself. . . ."

She covered her face with her hands. Tiny, gasping sobs came out.

It was darker outside. The oaks stood outlined against a cold twilight. There was a breeze; leaves pirouetted as they fell. The trees were multihued, lit glowingly by the failing sun. Kevin thought of Brahms.

A click sounded somewhere deep in the house. Outside, a light over the back porch came on. It was constricted, gave a spotlight of cold illumination for leaves to fall in.

In her chair, Eileen Connel moaned.

"My God!" She half rose out of her chair, pushed herself up weakly.

Lydia tried to coax her down. "Mother, sit—"

"Let me go, girl!" Eileen shouted. She lifted one weak arm to beat her daughter off. "Let go!" Her face was transfixed on the window.

"Is it me?" Kevin said, stepping back.

"No," Lydia replied. "She's been like this since yesterday."

Eileen Connel began a sound deep in her throat, a grief deeper than she had yet shown.

"No! My arm is so cold!" She reached out half blindly, took Kevin by the arm, tried to stand. "Oh, sweet Jesus, I almost remember!"

Sudden elation coursed through Kevin. He took Eileen Connel gently but firmly by the arm.

"What do you remember?" he coaxed.

"No! Oh, dear God, no!"

"Make her sit," Lydia said. "Where is that damned doctor!" She glanced out into the hallway.

"Tell me what you remember, Eileen," Kevin said.

"Oh, God!" Eileen clutched at Kevin's arm harder.

"Get her to sit down!" Lydia begged.

Kevin held on. Eileen brought her other hand up slowly. One trembling finger pointed toward the window. *"There,"* she said, breathing rapidly. Then, unexpectedly, her breathing steadied. A smile traced her lips.

"Chicken Little," she said.

"What does that mean?" Kevin said.

Eileen Connel's body relaxed. She sank back into her chair.

Then, once more, her body stiffened. Her hold on Kevin was viselike.

"I almost remember!" she cried.

"What is it?" Kevin said sharply.

"For heaven's sake, Kevin!" Lydia shouted, reaching for her mother's shoulder.

"Dammit, be quiet!" Kevin hissed.

"Ohhhhh," Eileen wailed.

"What is it?" Kevin whispered. "Tell me what you know!"

Eileen Connel's eyes widened in stark terror. Once again, her hand pointed straight out.

"Ohhh . . ."

"Tell me!"

She turned her eyes on Kevin, as if he were the window. "It's . . ."

Kevin shook her. "What!"

She wailed, pushed herself out of Kevin's grip. Lydia supported her as she fell into her chair. Eileen wept in little hiccups, shivering like a child.

Lydia quickly covered her with a quilted comforter. She

whispered into her ear, "Would you like some tea, Mother? Can I get you some tea?"

Eileen Connel relaxed. She turned her head to her daughter's breast and closed her eyes.

"Yes, Lydia, some tea . . ."

Lydia's eyes met Kevin's, with a fire in them he had never seen before.

"You son of a bitch."

"I'm sorry," Kevin said.

"All these years, that's all you wanted."

"Lydia—"

"You bastard. Didn't you know she was in love with you?"

The doorbell rang. Lydia rose, stepped toward him. She raised her hand and slapped his cheek. *"Get out,"* she said, and turned to answer the door.

The smell of lemon polish.

There was darkness in the corners of the house. Kevin heard the deep tocking of the grandfather clock, the high, insectlike ticking of the other clocks fighting to be heard.

Eileen Connel was asleep, her head nestled into the high winged corner of her chair. The comforter was snugged up below her face. She looked as peaceful as a child.

He walked to the sitting room, put on his coat. For a moment, he regarded the empty teacups side by side on the serving platter. A single light illumined the room. The piano gave him its wide, white smile by the doorway.

He didn't touch the keys. In the hallway, on the way out, he passed Dr. Carpenter, wrapped in a comforter, carrying his black bag, bending his head in whispered conversation with Lydia as they passed him without acknowledgment.

7

October 22nd

Three weeks.

Tired in his long bones, tired in his mind, James Weston could only think of happiness. It was like being a child again, after a day of running, playing ball, with the wide blue sky above him like a warming bowl, mown green grass underfoot, the smell of life itself in the air. Not a worry in the world; worries, indeed, unknown. He had forgotten what that felt like, a sensation that the universe was at your feet. There was a time in childhood, between cognition and the true age of reason, when nothing could hurt him. The world was a womb, and when that time was gone, something was gone forever.

But miraculously, James Weston had found it again these three weeks, picking apples under the warm autumn sun, with rolled flannel sleeves by noon, no shirt at all in the afternoon. Himself and the trees, which seemed to sing to him, breathe life into him, with their tired petals and red fruit, trunks that would soon sleep but not die. He had begun to see himself in the movie of his own mind again, and the movie was the healing of his own self. He had become as an apple tree, and it was time for his spring again. He was waking up into the daylight of his life again.

Only the nights had been troubled.

The first night in Ben Meyer's big guest bed was strange because he had not slept in a bed for so long. His back had grown accustomed to hard ground. He tossed all night, Rusty whimpering sympathy beside him, but his bones refused to sink into the soft beauty of the bed beneath. His dreams were chaotic, colorful bits of his journey from Vancouver to New York taped together, a spliced movie.

The second night, his body gave in to the softness of the bed, and he slept, but the dreams did not go away. They were with him all night, longer stretches of his trip, a home movie unreeling at high speed, endless hitchhiked rides, long, hot stretches of highway, dusty side roads, evenings under stars grown unnaturally bright. He slept fitfully. But between the work, and his body's sudden liking for the bed, he gained a useful if not full night's sleep.

Each night, though, the dreams grew worse, more vivid. It was as if he were a captive audience of an inner film over which he had no control. The twelfth night he dreamed of a snake he had seen in Wyoming, grown to monstrous proportions, lashing its rattled tail at the desert floor, throwing up mushrooms of dust as it sped toward him from the distance. There were black clouds under a sickly copper sky, raining dark-red blood. He tried to escape across a highway that dropped to a chasm under him, its centerline continuing forward, painted on air. As he fell, he awoke, clutching his sheets, searching frantically for purchase, not knowing where he was until Rusty jumped onto the bed, nuzzling him until his hands unclenched the sheets.

And so to this day, another in three weeks of good days, under an autumn sky of clear, deep sapphire, among living trees that seemed to breathe beneath his touch, pulling apples like tight-skinned uteri bearing the juice of life within, with Ben Meyer passing him, slapping him on the back, smiling on him like a father, and Ben's wife bringing lunches up to them from the house at the bottom of the hill, climbing slowly through the still frame of the movie that was this beautiful day, bearing a basket covered in blue-checked cloth, with sandwiches and a red-topped gray thermos with hot coffee inside, with pie and fruit and scraps for Rusty. As they ate, they watched Rusty and Ben's terrier, Rags, play, run around the apple trees, kick through dry leaves, with tall, wide cotton-ball clouds bearing majestically overhead from Vancouver to New York and beyond. New Polk was spread below them like a toy town, tall white church steeple, houses colored from a child's crayon box, blue and red and yellow, trees blotched yellow and brown and red; at the edge of the town the university like a town itself, a spread of green grass, perfect buildings, brown clocktower, white face, ebony arms; little cars moving through New Polk like toys; the day, the tart air, the clouds, the food, the work, the playing dogs, all of it making James drowsy, making him want to lay his long body down after Ben's wife gathered the remains of the lunch together and the day had grown long. Ben didn't seem set on going back to work. James put his back against a tree and put a long grass in his mouth, and Ben smoked, looked for a while at the sky and then at the retreating form of his wife taking the lunch and the dogs back to the house down the hill. He continued to watch as she tended her garden, moving her hoe lovingly through the rowed soil, a tiny figure in the midst of all that color, like a peasant in a Brueghel painting.

"This is a fine time of year," Ben said. He pulled in smoke from his pipe, let it drift from his mouth.

"I can see why you love it."

"If I could freeze a day like this, a moment like this, I could live in it forever."

James moved the grass from one corner of his mouth to the other.

Ben said, "Thank you for staying."

James looked at him. "I should be thanking you."

Ben shook his head. "It's not the work I'm talking about. I would have hired a couple of boys from town like I always do. The work gets done. I'm such a curmudgeon, they don't know if I'm alive or not in New Polk. It's more the companionship, and for Martha's sake. She's been kind of lonely, feeling it more, the last year or two."

James knew Ben would continue. He stretched one long leg out, leaned his head back against the tree.

"We had a boy," Ben said. "He died, a long time ago. We couldn't have another. There's been this hole in Martha's life, and now the hole seems to be getting bigger."

"What was his name?"

"Barry. He was seventeen, good at sports, liked to play ball. He was tall, like you. I was traveling a lot, then. When they got through to me, I was in Indiana. There was a fire, a whole bunch of kids at a Halloween party. We lost a whole class out of the high school, except for three. They said my boy died saving them."

Ben smoked his pipe, looked at the sky.

"I'm told you're supposed to let it go after a while. I don't know about that. I can't see his face so clear anymore. When I look at pictures of him, so sharp and focused, he looks like a stranger, somebody I knew when I was a boy. But in your heart, you never really forget. They take a piece of that with them. The hole never closes up again."

Ben smoked his pipe; James was silent.

"Sorry to go on like this," Ben said. "I just wanted you to know that you've filled up that hole for Martha a little. I can tell. She's happier lately, doing things for you and that dog of yours. The thing I wanted to ask you is, if you'd like to stay on a while longer . . ."

Ben had turned to regard the sky again; but James knew that Ben was waiting for him to speak.

"I've thought about it," James said. "It's been good for me, here. It's not only the relaxation, or the work. I ran away from a lot of things in California. Some of them I needed to run away from. There are people here in New York, my father down in the City, whom I need to see. After that, I don't know what I'm going to do."

"Like I told you . . ." Ben said.

James stretched, felt drowsiness coming over him. "It's funny," he said. "I don't even know why I came back to New York. I almost turned back halfway here. But something kept me going. It's like something made me keep going."

"Well . . ."

James looked up to see Ben standing over him, smiling. A tiredness, the sum of three weeks of bad sleep, the cool beauty of the day, the work behind him, the luxurious weakness of his muscles, the aftermath of the autumn lunch in his belly—all conspired to close his eyes.

"You sleep, son," Ben said. "Too nice a day to go back to work. Think about what I said."

James nodded; through closing eyes, he vaguely saw the trail of Ben's smoke as he walked away, descended the hill. The day became a blanket around him; the hard back of the tree was the hard ground he had grown used to, the sounds of the trees were lullabies. He closed his eyes . . .

.   .   .

The heat. He was in Iowa, summer, and everything he had heard was true. The land was flat as a griddle around him, the fields bleached yellow, corn ticking like dry sticks. He had not seen water, a running stream, the gurgling wetness of a creek, the blue, flat mirror of a puddle, for two days. Dry highway was what he had seen—an endless stretch of flat, gray-black road, edged in dust, from the cabs of a succession of trucks. And now, toward the end of the day, the trucks had stopped, the highway stretched empty ahead of him, and he was thirsty.

What the hell am I doing?

The last couple of days, he had begun to wonder. Since he had hit the heat of the Midwest, had come face-to-face with real summer, the idea that he had made his point, had been foolish enough, had begun to take root. And after another day of parched hitchhiking, through a vast, flat hell of corn-filled nothingness, he had all but decided he had had enough.

Marcie would be worried about him by now, and Samuels would be frantic. Three weeks. He supposed it had taken Marcie this long to come around; but Samuels, he would wager, had begun to go crazy after two days. After all, James had disappeared before, marching petulantly off a miniseries set once because he didn't like his trailer. But that had been three years ago, and James's prima-donna days were supposedly behind him. There had been fights since, but he had never walked off another job. Or disappeared as one was about to begin.

That's what would have Samuels going, the fact that James was due in Burbank in ten days for a movie shoot. Six weeks beyond that, he had a recurring character part in a midseason television replacement. And a running shoe ad to shoot in late September. And then—

James figured Marcie had been able to hold Samuels off from calling the FBI until now. After all, James and Marcie's normal fights had been big enough for at least a week's cool-

ing-off period. They had never gone at it quite so viciously as this before. And even at the end, after a night straight out of Who's Afraid of Virginia Wolfe, raging through the Vancouver trailer, by the end of which he had brought up Marcie's long-dead coke dependency and she had pulled two or three of his old lovers out of the scrapbook, they both knew that the point of exhaustion had been passed, that they had fought as hard as they could and would eventually patch it up. In a way it had been exhilarating, knowing that this was as bad as it could get. He almost threatened her with a knife. But he knew that if he did, she would only laugh and he would end up laughing, too, and that would be the end of it. He needed to go a little further than that, to make a point.

So, the next day, after the wrap of the shoot on the Lincoln movie, he had simply walked out and kept walking.

At first it was a joke, his wearing the Lincoln costume and all. And then it became serious, after Marcie passed him in her Corvette on the way out of town and shouted, "Watch out for John Wilkes Booth, shithead!" before roaring off.

So he kept walking. And after a day of it, it had seemed like a good idea to just keep going. Because some thoughts had begun to grow in his head, and it occurred to him that this was as good a time as any to attend to them.

So he had begun the Great Walk, and seen the country, and almost no one recognized him, even with his Lincoln getup, and for a while it was just fine.

Then he got to Iowa.

Maybe it was something about the approaching Mississippi River. In his mind, over the weeks of his travel, it had become a sort of dividing line between seriousness and frivolity. Twice he had caught himself in telephone booths, quarter dropped into slot, area code and six of Marcie's seven digits dialed. His momentum had flagged. He was getting tired.

He didn't really want to go back East.

That, he knew, was the real issue. If he crossed the Missis-

sippi, he had made a pact with his heart that he would go all
the way, complete the Great Walk, and settle things once and
for all in New York. Marcie he wasn't worried about; he had
begun to miss her terribly, but he knew she would come to
understand what he had done and why. She would understand that it had nothing to do with her, really, and that it
was something he would have had to do anyway. His agent he
could handle; the lost work would go to someone else in the
stable. It might hurt him for six months, but they would start
asking him to do this part, that part, again. The tabloid lies
might even help fuel the fire of his popularity.

So, the issue: Did he want to go on? If he crossed the
Mississippi, he would have to face his past. There was no other
reason to continue.

Suddenly, standing on this heat-baked ribbon of highway
in Iowa, with the smell of the big river almost to his nostrils,
with the dry, brittle, motionless, chest-high fields of corn
around him, he knew that he didn't want to go on, that it
wasn't time to face his past yet.

He would return to California.

He would hitch a ride to Cedar Rapids, call Marcie from
the airport, get the first connecting flight to Los Angeles, and
be back in L.A. by tomorrow.

The Great Walk, for now, was over.

A constriction lifted from his heart. The sun was lowering,
but he felt it rising within him, bringing peace to the region of
his heart. When he thumbed a ride and got into a glossy,
huge Peterbilt that stopped for him, he leaned back and immediately slept, until the driver pushed him gently awake on
the shoulder.

"Buddy, time for you to get out."

James blinked awake into the sun at the horizon. It was
nearly twilight.

"We in Cedar Rapids?"

"I can get you there tomorrow, if you want. I been hauling

six nights straight, got to get off the pills 'fore I run her off the road."

"Where are we?" For the first time James looked at the driver's face: a burned-out mess, the reddest eyes he had ever seen. Cap pushed back, beard stubble, a heavy-set man with a kind but tired face.

The driver blinked awake. "Wish I could sleep you here, but there's only room for one. I noticed some lights ahead. Sorry, I've really got to crash. Meet me in the morning."

As James climbed down, the driver was already slumping over, pulling a blanket over himself as he lay across the front seats.

James stretched. The sun had dropped below the horizon. The night was summer warm, dotted with pinhole stars, a humid breeze. The ever-present corn had begun to rustle, grumbling in the dark. He heard a low, mechanical rumble. A glow of light sat like a beetle in the darkness ahead.

A mile's walk and he reached it. A carnival, its last night here, according to the roadside banner, ennui already setting in. Red and white signs, lots of exclamation points, a few desultory customers padding the beaten dirt paths among faded-paint rides. Orange metal fencing around them. Turning teacups, gray, with a blue stripe around the top, a Ferris wheel whose apex dipped up into the night, a merry-go-round with a few squealing children, hot-looking parents waiting, bored for it to end. The calliope missed a few bars of Schubert's "Marche Militaire," an intermittent hollow chunk where a tinkly note should be.

James bought a cola, syrupy warm, at a dull-red kiosk, thought on a whim of trying to win a Kewpie doll for Marcie. The bottles he had to knock over were dented, battleship colored; the balls rubbed with dirt, old, soft around the seams. All but one bottle fell from its base. On his second try he cleared them all, was handed a small doll, orange, spiky hair, wide-awake eyes, frightening grin. It had flat pieces of red felt for hands and feet. One side seam was torn, showing cheap padding, walnut-shell pieces.

He was suddenly depressed. He was about to put the doll in a nearby metal oil-drum trash container, saw an empty-handed little girl staring at him, and handed it to her.

"Look, Daddy!" she cried, running to her father a few paces away. The father stood mopping his hairline with a tired handkerchief. "Look what I won! What about my cotton candy?"

The father looked down at her, nodded tired thanks to James, drew the little girl away toward a nearby booth where an aluminum pan churned pink, threadlike sugar around long, fragile white paper cones.

At eleven, the small crowd dispersed. James followed them to a square, dusty parking lot cornered with long poles topped by red pennants. Strings of red and white Christmas lights sagged between the poles. Some of the bulbs were out; one white one blinked annoyingly, on and off.

James stopped a man who was just helping his wife into their station wagon. A little boy was curled on the back seat, thumb in mouth, clutching a stuffed tiger. The tiger had the same frightening smile as the Kewpie doll.

"Can you tell me where the nearest town is?" James asked.

The man turned languidly to him. He flicked a mosquito away from his ear, scratched at his sweaty neck around the back. He wore a checked, short-sleeved sport shirt, was thin, with thinning hair. "Jeez, there ain't a town near here. Nearest one's forty miles away. This is farming country, if you haven't noticed." He smiled tiredly.

"Is there anywhere I could find lodging for the night?"

The man looked him up and down, stifled a yawn. "Sorry, no, mister." He closed the door to his wife's side, walked around, got into his car. Without another word he pulled the station wagon out, drove off.

All the cars drove off.

The string lights in the parking lot blinked once, in unison with the one defective bulb, then went out. James heard the pennant at the top of one of the corner poles flap lazily. The calliope stopped. Far off, over the fields, corn murmured.

Most of the booths and kiosks had been abandoned. There was a small show tent, green-and-white-striped, faded. James entered. Inside was a minuscule stage, two steps up, pine planking, knotholes fallen out from dryness. Facing it was a half circle of thirty or forty folding chairs.

A man in clown makeup and ballooning red-and-white suit sat on one of the chairs in the last row, hunched over a makeup box. His head was completely white save for a crowning, monklike fringe of bright red hair. James was reminded of the Kewpie doll.

"What—?" The clown swiveled with surprise toward James, as if he had been caught at something. James was relieved to see that his mouth, which had been cleaned of makeup, did not have the Kewpie-doll grin he had seen so often that evening.

"Sorry," James apologized.

"Sure." The clown rustled in his makeup box before turning back to James. There was a small rectangular mirror set in the open, hinged cover of the box.

"You lost?" the clown said, his tone cool.

"Guess I am. I've been hitchhiking. My ride dropped me here for the night."

The clown studied him. "That getup, I thought you were part of the show."

James smiled. "It's a long story."

"So tell it to me," the clown said. Abruptly he rose, walked to the stage, reached behind it. He pulled out a large blue metal cooler. Grunting with effort, he dragged it around to the front of the stage. He opened it, fished into water, produced two beer cans before slamming the cooler shut.

"*Alfresco,*" he said, tossing one of the beer cans underhand to James.

"*Thanks.*" The beer was cold; when it went down, it tasted even colder. James remembered how warm in comparison his cola had been.

The clown sat on the cooler, feet spread apart, arms on his knees, dangling the beer from one hand. He studied the ground before he looked up. "I'm Billy Peters. You're . . . ?"

"James Weston."

"They call you Jimmy?"

"No."

"Fine." A tentative smile. "So how do you like our little outfit, James?"

"Well—"

"Tell me the truth. Sucks, doesn't it? You know what it's like trying to make a buck in carnivals today? Especially an old *carnival?*"

Before James could answer, the clown said, "Can't be done." He straightened, put the beer to his mouth, drank, lowered the can. "This is the third outfit I've been with in three years." Again he drank from the beer can. "Just can't be done."

"I was wondering why there were so few people here tonight. With not much happening around here, and this being the last night, you'd think—"

The clown waved his hand. "They would have been here. Would have packed the place. There's nothing to do here but screw dogs or sit on corn. They had a multiple murder here couple days ago, that's why they weren't here."

The clown waved his hand again. "Happens all the time. You know how these farm families are. Dad tells Sonny he can't whack off anymore in the outhouse, or can't go out with Betty Sue 'cause Dad wants to bop her himself, so late one night, Sonny gets the Winchester Dad gave him for his twelfth *birthday out of the garage, spends an hour up in his room cleaning, oiling, and loading it, then walks calmly into Mom and Dad's room, blows their heads off, does the same to Sis and Junior, then sucks the barrel like an El Producto and meets 'em all in heaven." The clown looked down at his beer. "Happens every week. Farmer roulette."*

James sipped from his own beer. The clown emptied his, stood to open the cooler lid and fish for another beer. He resumed his place.

"So," Billy Peters said after sampling the new beer, "what's your story?"

James told him an edited version. He admitted that he was hitchhiking across the country on a whim. "But now," he said, "I think it's time to head back to L.A."

"You were going to New York?" the clown asked.

James nodded. "Grew up there."

"Ah." The clown sucked on his beer.

"I wanted to ask you," James said, "if there was a place I could sleep tonight."

"Sure," the clown said. He smiled, an odd thing, the top of his face covered in white makeup, wide, exaggerated eyes, bright white, the bottom containing his all-too-normal grin. He drained his beer, stood, brought two more cold ones out of the cooler. He tossed one to James, the same smooth underhand motion. "One more beer and I'll set you up."

Forty minutes later, the beer slowing his mind, lulling his already tired body, James Weston followed Billy Peters to his camp wagon. They passed a couple of roustabouts in the darkness, laughing, passing a wine bottle, talking about sleeping late the next morning before breaking down.

There wasn't enough room inside the wagon for two. It was covered in litter, old girlie magazines, empty Styrofoam coffee cups, beer cans, clothing, makeup supplies. It smelled musty.

The blanket Peters handed him was stained, flakes of paper adhering to it. Peters made no apology, removed his costume, lay on his lumpy bed in his skivvies, turned his head to the wall.

James went outside. He shook the blanket out, lay on the ground, covered himself. He heard vague sounds, far off, a hoot of laughter. There was a cross of stars directly overhead. Cygnus, the Swan. The Northern Cross. He closed his eyes.

And instantly opened them. The clown, Billy Peters, was on top of him, his mouth opened so wide it looked as if it had been repainted. The clown made little gurgling sounds deep in the back of his throat.

James tried to throw the clown off. He was pinned at shoulders and arms. Peters put large hands on James's face, palms flat, conforming to the contours of James's cheeks. With his thumbs, he pressed down under James's chin, above the Adam's apple, cutting off air.

James thrashed, thought of the nearby roustabouts, tried to shout. He could make no sound, could barely breathe. Billy Peters's face lowered. James's vision was beginning to swim. The clown's fingers, pressed hard on his face, were forcing his mouth open, pulling the teeth apart, holding them open like clamps.

The sounds in the back of the clown's throat, a rasping grate, became louder. James had the feeling that the clown was about to put his mouth over James's and kiss him. The clown's eyes were unnaturally large, bloodshot, his breath oddly cold.

James began to black out. The rasping sound became huge in his ears, with a rush of blood, and as the clown lowered his mouth, James saw in his failing sight something small and grayish appear on the clown's tongue—a movement of antennae or legs, which fell. He felt it scrape the back of his own throat. Immediately, he felt a freezing cold.

With a gargantuan effort, convulsing with lack of oxygen,

choking, he threw Billy Peters aside. James held his hands to his neck, pulling oxygen in, and at the same time, trying to expel the thing in his throat. He felt it digging, finding purchase. Then there was an excruciating pain, as if a huge dentist's needle had been driven up into the back of his throat, filling it with numbing, icy novocaine.

He tried to scream. An airy, nearly inaudible hiss came out. He threw himself on the ground, clawing at the dirt. His mind was blind with pain. He saw fire in front of his eyes, felt as if his entire head was burning in acid. None of the thing's movements in the back of his throat were lost to him: he felt each tiny, boring cut, each movement of tiny legs, as it angled up—

Then, in a flash of blindness that left him gasping, the pain was gone.

The sudden release from cold fire was like an orgasm. James fell back on the ground, gulping for air. His sight cleared, and as he blinked the tears of pain out of his eyes, he saw that the Northern Cross had wheeled toward the west, its trailing stars hidden by the cutting corner of the top of the camper.

As his breathing evened, he heard Billy Peters gasping.

James sat up. The clown was convulsing mightily. He had crawled to the front of the camper, and his hands clutched the front tire. His body was racked with shooting spasms. James stood, approached him.

The clown's body gave off a hissing sound, like air escaping a punctured balloon.

James pressed the toe of his boot into the clown's shoulder and turned him on his back. Billy Peters's hands let go of the tire. He fell back, twitching. His head, a grotesque mask, half man, half clown, hit repeatedly on the dirt.

Hsssssssssss, the body said.

Billy Peters's mouth tried to speak; he tried to raise his hand.

Hsssssssssss.

The eyes dropped away. The face collapsed like a sand castle dried in the sun. The body crumbled within its clothes.

The skull fell back against the ground, then turned, in one hissing moment, to a pile of dust.

James lifted the clothes. Dust spilled out of them. There was a sound like sand running through fingers. A plume of fine particles drifted away.

From the far side of the carnival site, James heard a roustabout's curt laughter.

Beyond, he heard the hissing of corn, like the sound of the disappearing man.

James shook the clothes out, threw them in the trailer, closed the door, walked away.

He walked, until the dim night-lights of the carnival were a mile behind. The looming rectangle of the trailer truck he had left grew off the highway. When he reached the cab of the truck, he stopped walking.

He lay down off the road next to the truck and slept.

He dreamed he wore a clown face, and was climbing into the open window of a farmhouse with a Winchester rifle. He emptied the house of life, lastly a boy in a room covered with baseball pennants and trophies, the blue barrel of the rifle in the boy's mouth, below his ruined head, carefully wrapping the dead hands around it before they stiffened. Then he dreamed that he was a man who repaired telephones, and a woman who sold cosmetics door-to-door, and a man who lived alone in the mountains but who sometimes came down into town, to visit a lone woman who would then die, or meet someone on a lone road with snow falling, who was later found tripped into a bear trap, head nearly severed. He was another man and then another, and a woman and a little girl, and another man who liked to collect stamps and worked at a nursing home where many old people died.

And, finally, he was a little boy who lived in a town where apples grew.

Yes, he said in his dream, and he didn't know if the words had come from his own mouth.

He slept, dreamless.

In the morning, the dreams were forgotten. The truck driver, stubbled but rested, once again poked him awake, saying it was time to go.

And when James got up and stretched, he realized that he wanted to go on with his quest after all, that this was surely the time to finish what he had started, to go back East. Marcie and his work, and Samuels, would just have to wait.

He felt rejuvenated. They were on the road immediately, passing a roadside carnival breaking down that looked vaguely familiar to James. But his eyes looked away from it, to the highway.

He bought the truck driver breakfast in Cedar Rapids. They talked, and laughed, and James found himself watching the truck driver leave with regret, going into the lonely confines of the back of his truck to check that his load was tied down, as James clutched his knife a little too hard over his eggs, and had to pry it curiously from his fingers with his other hand.

No, he said to himself, and found that curious, and disconcerting, because he didn't feel as if he had really said it.

But he felt much better when he walked out into the sunny morning and breathed the air, and found a shaggy red setter in the parking lot, an abandoned dog with nowhere to go who checked him over once and then held back.

Go ahead, that disconcerting voice in the back of his head said to him. Take him with you. I don't need you yet.

"Here, boy," he said, smiling at the dog, and the setter soon came to him and stayed.

"Good boy. I'll call you Rusty. Want to go to New York?"
The dog barked once.
"Good."
James put his thumb out, pointing east . . .

"James?"
Once again, someone poked him. His mind's movie fast-forwarded, past the dream, to the present. Up at the top of his throat, something stirred, stretched, threw tendrils out. He could feel it taking hold of the projector, loading a new spool of film into it, not his own.
Now I need you.
James opened his eyes.

Ben Meyer was there, smiling down at him. James heard huffing, saw Rusty and Rags regarding him.

James stretched his arms up high over his head. He smiled. "Lord, how long did I sleep?"

"Sun's going down," Ben said. "Past suppertime. If you slept any longer, I would have had to throw a blanket over you, leave you to the cold."

James stood up, felt his cracking bones align, make him tall.

His foot, he discovered, was asleep; he stumbled forward, almost lost his balance. Ben Meyer grabbed his arm, steadied him.

"Heavens, boy, you're cold as ice. Let's get you down to the house."

Rusty regarded James curiously, head cocked to one side.

James put his hand down to the dog's head, scratched behind the ears. "Don't worry, boy, it's just me."

The dog huffed.

Now.

They walked out of the apple orchard, down the gentle grassed slope of the hill. It was late in the day. The sun had painted the west orange. Overhead, the fattening sickle of the coming hunter's moon was brightening, from pale yellow to bold amber. They could see their breath as they walked. Below, the farmhouse pushed a thin line of trailing smoke from its brick chimney.

"Martha!" Ben called as they set their feet on the curling stoned walk to the front porch. "Martha, get a tub ready!"

On the front porch, leaning solidly against the doorpost, was Martha's hoe, its blade lipped with dirt.

As Ben mounted the porch, James lifted the hoe in both hands, raised it blade side up.

Ben reached to open the door, and James brought the hoe down on the back of his head.

The lip of dried dirt flew in a neat line from the edge of the hoe. James heard the rushing-breath, surprised little sound that Ben made. Ben collapsed to his knees, hands groping. James planted his feet, raised the hoe. Ben was reaching for the back of his neck when James hit him again, a stronger blow.

There was only the sound of the curved metal fastener between hoe and wooden handle hitting Ben's skull. James brought the hoe down again. The flat blade broke free, leaving the fastener intact, looking like a curled metal finger.

The dogs began to howl. James turned to them. Rusty backed away on his haunches, ears flattened back, barking fiercely.

"Come here, boy," James said.

Inside the house there was commotion. James heard Martha walking the creaking floorboards to the front hallway. "What's all this about?" she said.

James took a quick step off the porch. He feinted a blow at Rusty, then struck out at Rags, who had stayed on the edge of the porch. The blow caught the dog in the left eye. Rags yelped, backed off the porch into the dirt. James followed. A short, hard thrust and the dog lay still.

James faced Rusty, who had backed farther away.

"Come here," he said.

The dog made a deep, growling sound.

The front door of the house opened, and Rusty turned and ran.

James quickly mounted the porch steps. As Martha's eyes registered Ben lying in a pool of blood, James drove her back with the hoe into the front hallway. She let out a broken cry. She fell onto the floor inside, and the screen door closed between them. James ripped it viciously open. Martha sought to rise and failed.

James brought the instrument down, a long sliding curve to the side of her head. Martha's eyes unfocused. He hit her again. A burp of blood spotted her tongue.

As the weapon rounded again on her, she locked her eyes on James and cried out, *"Barry!"*

He struck her once more, and she was silent.

James marched out onto the porch to look for the dog. It was nearly dark. He thought he saw Rusty up the slope, heading for the apple orchard, but he could not be sure. There was not enough moonlight to hunt by. The dog would have to wait.

In the barn, James found an electric Coleman lantern and a shovel. He set the lantern at the tilled edge of the garden and turned it on.

Its twin neon rods flashed to low, blue-white brilliance.

He dug two deep, wide holes, eight feet apart. He dragged the two bodies from the house. He threw Rags and the broken hoe pieces into the hole with Martha, spaded dirt into the holes, spread the remaining dirt over the rest of the tilled area. He worked on it for a long time, until it looked just as it had before.

Where he had hit Rags near the porch there was blood. By lantern light, on his hands and knees, he dusted it into the dirt.

There were stains on the porch and in the front hallway. He scrubbed them out. Then he put the lantern and shovel away and went into the house.

There was a low fire in the wood stove in the living room. He stoked it. He began to shiver. He heard a sound: his teeth chattering.

He lay down on the couch, head on one stiff arm, and stared at the ceiling.

He did not close his eyes.

Somewhere deep in the night, when it was coldest, he heard the mournful bark of a dog and said, not with his own voice, "Yes, I'm back."

BOOK TWO

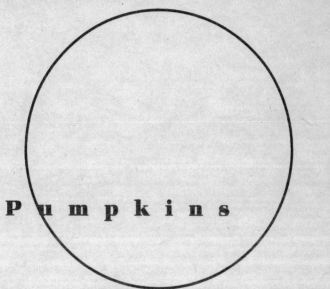

Pumpkins

8

October 22nd

Davey Putnam watched the black-and-white police cruiser stop in front of the house from his second-story window. He hoped for a moment it would continue on, pull away from the curb. But the door on the driver's side angled open and the crew-cut, square frame of Officer Johnston got out.

"Damn," Davey said.

Below him, he heard the front door open. He saw his foster father come down the walk halfway to meet the cop.

"What is it now?" ole Jack yelled.

"In the house, please," Johnston replied, and firmly, the cop got him to turn around and bring the argument into the house.

Argument it was. Davey went to the hole in the floorboards next to his bed, where a cable-TV hole had once been drilled for the former owners. He couldn't hear what was going on below. They had moved into the back of the house, probably the kitchen.

Davey got up, opened the door to his room a crack. He heard the low, unintelligible voice of the cop. Then he heard ole Jack nearly shout, "I don't care if the kid's old man tried to have you fired! That's between you and him! Stop getting on my ass about it!"

That was all he heard for a while. Occasionally, there was the thin, piping rasp of The Mouth, her mousy, annoying whine contrasting with the two male voices. Johnston was talking long and even. After a while he was doing all the talking.

After twenty minutes or so Davey heard Officer Johnston say, "All right." He heard the cop approach the front door and leave. Davey went to the window and watched Johnston get into his black-and-white, rev the engine, pull sharply out from the curb.

Davey sat on the bed and watched the sweep second hand on the old electric clock next to his bed. He thought of it as a game. The longest it had ever taken for them to call him after the cops had come was four minutes and fifteen seconds.

Five minutes went by, and nothing happened.

He went to the door, opened it again, listened. A scraping sound, a snatch of a weak hum. The Mouth in the kitchen, getting dinner ready.

Where was ole Jack?

Davey heard the back door creak open. He heard ole Jack say, "Where the fuck is that other beer?"

Timidly, The Mouth said, "That was the last one. I *told* you."

"The hell it was! I bought two extra, there were only eight! Now where the hell is the last one!"

"Jack, there were seven—"

"That kid take it? Get the little fucker down—"

He heard The Mouth protest, heard the refrigerator door bang open, bottles rattle. She was probably moving things around desperately. The only way to avoid the beating was to find the beer. "Maybe you're right, Jack," she whimpered. "Maybe you're right—"

Then, a bray of triumph from ole Jack. "You dumb slut! Right here on the door shelf! I *told* you there were eight!"

The refrigerator door slammed shut. The back door slammed open and shut, ole Jack proclaiming The Mouth's stupidity. After a moment of whimpering, The Mouth returned to the scraping sound of preparing dinner.

The back door creaked open again, flew closed with a bang. Ole Jack yelled, *"Where is he!"*

"Jack—" The Mouth began.

"Where is the little bastard! Get him down here!"

The tone in his voice told Davey this was not something she could talk him out of. They all knew the drill. There were levels to ole Jack's violence, and this was near the top. A quick flare of fuse had been lit, reached the bomb in no time. When that powder went off, everybody got burned.

"I said get him down here!"

Davey heard the giving, hard slap of flesh against flesh, heard The Mouth's whimpering cut to a sudden cry, followed by moans. Another slap. Ole Jack cursed, grunting with each blow he gave her. His voice vibrated in cadence with the hits: "WHERE—THE—FUCK—IS—HE!"

Between her whimpers she said, "Up . . . stairs . . . he's . . . upstairs . . ."

Davey heard her gasp as ole Jack left off hitting her. Ole Jack tramped down the hallway, approached the stairs. Davey saw the small, balding head appear above the floorline before he slammed the door shut and put his weight against it.

Ole Jack hit the door hard. It gave an inch before Davey reclosed it.

Ole Jack yelled, grunted against the door again.

Davey kept his weight on the door, digging his sneakers into the nicked floorboards.

"Shit!" ole Jack yelled. The pressure eased against the door. Davey stepped back away as ole Jack hit the door full force. The door flew open, and ole Jack fell into the room.

Davey bolted for the doorway. He was out into the hall before a heavy hand fell on his shoulder. He was pulled back into the bedroom. His foster father put both hands on him, turned him around, held him tight on the shoulder blades.

"You think that's *funny?*" Ole Jack was panting, face sweaty. "Answer me!"

"Fuck you," Davey said. By whipping his head back, he was able to deflect partially the first slap.

Quick blows with narration followed: "You—little—fucker—calling—me—that."

Davey threw up an arm finally, warding off a blow. He struck his foster father smartly on the nose.

"Jesus!" ole Jack said. He pulled his hands away from Davey, covered his nose.

The Mouth appeared in the doorway. As Davey backed away, she took hold of him, yelling at ole Jack, "That's enough! Leave the boy alone!"

"He broke my nose!" ole Jack screamed. He sat down heavily on Davey's bed, touched his nose tenderly. His hands were covered in blood.

"Don't you—" The Mouth began.

Ole Jack reached into his shirt pocket. He pulled out a bottle cap stamped GENESEE. "I found this in the backyard!" he whined accusingly. "The boy's been drinking. Ask him!" He rose menacingly, winced at the pain in his nose, sat down again, covered his nose with his hands. "Shit!"

"Come with me," The Mouth said to Davey. She dropped her thin arm around his shoulder, drew him out of the room, glancing at her husband to make sure he hadn't risen from the bed.

She brought Davey into the bathroom, closed and locked the door, put the toilet seat cover down, sat him on it, made him turn his face up toward the light.

"He smacked you good," she said.

Her own face was puffy, her hair stringy, a red mark turning black under one eye.

"He's a bastard," Davey said.

She paused in her ministrations, stared down at him. "He can't help it."

"I hate him."

She took a soiled washcloth from its rack next to the sink, ran cold water over it. She dabbed at the marks on his face, flinching. "You really popped him good," she said, smiling mischievously. "Good thing he already had his beer, or he'd be on us now. I bet he's asleep by now. If we're lucky, he'll forget about it in the morning."

As she rubbed at a long bruise on his left temple, Davey held her hand away. "Why was that cop here?"

"That?" she said dismissively. "The goddamned Reileys next door complained again. Said Jack wasn't taking care of the lawn. Property values. You think this was goddamned Society Hill."

"That was all?"

Her face showed surprise. "Why?" Her dim eyes held focus. "Have you done something?"

"No," he said quickly. "I was just wondering."

She rubbed a final time at a scratch under his eye, tossed the washcloth in the sink. "Come on," she said.

She unlocked the bathroom door, opened it to look out. Tentatively, she went out into the hall and approached Davey's bedroom.

Ole Jack was sprawled on Davey's bed, asleep. One hand

lay protectively over his nose; a few spots of blood dotted the top sheet.

"He'll be out all night," The Mouth said. "We'll be okay."

Davey looked at ole Jack's prone form, said, "Bastard."

After a dinner of SpaghettiOs, with Ring Dings for dessert, a glass of water for Davey, a half bottle of red table wine for The Mouth, she told him to go to sleep. She climbed the stairs to her bedroom, leaving Davey the couch in the living room and a frayed, dusty-blue afghan. He stripped to his shorts, left the television on, dozed off in front of it.

Soon after, he was awakened. He tensed, thinking it was ole Jack descending.

"Shhhh," The Mouth said. She knelt beside the couch. "It's uncomfortable down here. Come up to the big bed."

"No."

"Fine," she said.

She lifted the afghan, snuggled her small body up against his, groped into his shorts.

"No!" Davey said. He pushed against her, dropped her off the couch.

"It's okay, Davey," she whimpered. "It's okay." She tried to climb back next to him.

He lashed out at her with his arm.

"Stay away!"

She sat back on the floor, looked helplessly around.

"Davey—"

"What the fuck is *wrong* with you?" Davey shouted. He got up, moved away from her, around the couch. "This isn't the way it's supposed to be! You people are *sick!*"

He grabbed his clothes, clutched them to his chest, stumbled from the room. He saw her get up and follow him.

"Stay away from me!"

She stopped. He mounted the stairs two at a time, went into the bathroom, locked the door.

He sat on the toilet seat cover, hands balled into his eyes, rocking. Finally, he let big, long sobs rise from inside, burst out.

Later, when he had stopped crying, he dressed and went out into the hallway. The door to The Mouth's bedroom was closed.

He went into his room, past the snoring form of ole Jack. There was an envelope in the back of his desk drawer, and he pulled it out, jamming it into his back pocket.

He dismounted the stairs, found his jacket, put it on, and left the house.

He walked through his old neighborhood, collar up, jacket zipped to his throat. After a while, he began to feel the chill of the night.

There were fallen leaves pooled under the streetlights. His feet made them jump away as he walked through them. Many of the houses had Halloween decorations up, uncarved pumpkins on their stoops and porches.

He remembered this street on Halloween when he was five years old. His mother had dressed him like a clown. They walked from house to house. He vaguely remembered the feel of his mother's hand covering his, keeping his hand warm. He remembered feeling vaguely cold through the clown costume.

He remembered the porch lights. Every house had a carved pumpkin. One was so big it needed a table to rest on. Its eyes were cut like diamonds, its nose a triangle. Another pumpkin had a large O for a mouth, with teeth on the bottom, candle fire dancing inside.

He remembered crying.

"Davey, you okay?"

He remembered his mother's face, brushing her combed hair back when she bent down to him. She smelled like perfume water. He remembered the yellow boxes of perfume water on her dressing table.

He pointed at the O mouth of the pumpkin.

"Oh, Davey," she said, hugging him.

He shivered through his costume. "Like the fire burning up the children."

"Who told you that story?" she asked.

He began to cry.

"The big kids?" she asked. "Did they tell you that?"

He nodded against her.

"Davey, that happened a long long time ago. There's nothing for you to be afraid of."

"They'll burn *you* up."

"Oh, Davey!" She hugged him, held him away, looked into his eyes solemnly. "Nothing's going to happen to me."

He looked at her, lip quivering.

"Davey," she said, pulling him close to her again. "I promise, I'll always be here."

"You promise?"

"Yes, I promise . . ."

But six years later she broke her promise, his mother and father were dead, and it was all gone, his childhood, his father, his mother, the fall of her hair, the smell of perfume water . . .

He began to cry again. When he cleared his eyes, he found he had stopped in front of the house he had lived in. The shutters were no longer red, but in the dark, the house looked the same.

His house.

He tried to make himself stop crying. He wasn't supposed to act like this. He was sixteen, he was tough. But he couldn't stop. He felt himself bisected, an earlier self stuck here in this place, in this house, in happiness, faraway reality. If he had never had it, he knew he would not be missing it. He would get along, had learned to be tough. But he had had that other life, had known what it was like to be happy, and he wanted it back.

Perfume water, her hand covering his, the long fingers cold . . .

"It's not supposed to be like this!"

He began to sob again. Only when the porch light went on in the house where he had lived, illuminating a door that had been painted red but was now a dull green, a different door to a different world—only when that light went on, throwing light on the new real world, a circle of light on a pumpkin, drawn face, a round O with teeth for a mouth, did he wipe his palms into his eyes and run on.

Deep in the night, he watched the moon swim up over him for company. On the edge of the park, where he thought he might sleep on one of the benches, he saw the outline of a patrol car just before he would have been seen. The lit end of a cigarette flared like a coal; he heard the cop cough and then spit.

He circled out of the park, found himself eventually at the outskirts of town. If he reversed and walked east, he would come to the university. The grounds were patrolled by security, making it impossible for sleep.

He walked on, grew tired, cut up away from the well-traveled road, crested the top of a hill, looking for a good place to rest. He followed the line of the ridge.

A trim line of trees appeared in the moonlight before him. He was in one of the apple orchards that encircled New Polk like beads. He thought he knew this one. He climbed a low rock wall and suddenly was in the midst of trees. The tart-sweet smell of apples filled his nostrils. He could not walk without stepping on fruit. He searched for and finally found a relatively intact apple, eating it as he walked.

As he reached the heart of the orchard, the moon was shadowed by a tree limb.

Davey heard a sound.

He stood still, listened.

There it was—a low growl in the back of an animal's throat.

The sound went away, then came again, close by—a throaty growl with an undercurrent of fright.

Davey eyed the nearby ranks of trees, saw nothing.

Slowly, Davey lowered himself to one knee. He clicked his tongue. "Here, boy. Come on, let's have a look."

The growl came, followed by a tentative, hoarse bark.

"Come on, boy."

To Davey's right, the form of a large red setter walked out of tree shadow into moonlight. Davey let the dog study him, sniffing, moving its head from side to side.

The dog huffed, more robustly.

"Come here," Davey urged.

The dog advanced. Davey cupped his hand. The dog nuzzled into it, sniffing and then licking, making a whining sound deep in its throat.

"What's the matter? Somebody beat you?"

Slowly, Davey went over the dog. He found no bruises, but discovered that the dog loved to be scratched behind the ears, deep into his coat.

"You lost? Run away?"

The dog had no collar or tags.

"Road dog, right? Want to stick with me?"

The dog huffed, nuzzled into his hand, up his arm.

"Just one thing I've got to check."

Davey continued through the trees. The dog lingered, made a mournful sound. Davey stopped, urged the dog forward, waited till it was at his side.

Davey made his way through the last block of trees to the edge of the orchard.

Where the trees ended, he stopped and looked down the hillside. The moon was high up, perfectly placed for seeing.

The lights in the farmhouse below were lit. Davey was sure of his location now—Ben Meyer's orchard. He and Buddy had picked apples for Meyer once. The old man had a reputation as a loner and a grouch, but they had been treated just fine, and the old woman had doted on them.

But this was not Ben Meyer in the yard. A tall man in shirt and suspenders was cleaning something in front of the porch. He was down on his hands and knees in the dirt. When he was finished, he went to the porch and began to scrub it. Then he brought his cleaning utensils into the house. Davey could make out the tall man's form moving around inside the screen door.

"You're afraid of him?" Davey asked the dog.

The dog whined, gave a low bark.

Davey watched the man continue his work. After a while, the man came out of the house, went to the barn, then returned to the house. All the lights stayed on.

"Okay, boy, let's go."

Davey retreated deep into the orchard. He found a flat area, covered with leaves and grass, under a tree that filtered the moonlight. He cleared it of fallen apples. The dog sat on its haunches, tongue lolling, and watched him.

He lay down, hands behind his head.

"Come here, boy," he said.

The dog growled.

"What's the matter? Don't want to stay here?"

In answer, the dog whined.

Davey held his hand out. After a moment, the dog let him scratch it behind the ears, settling close by.

"Tomorrow we'll go. Okay?"

The dog let out a long breath that sounded like a sigh.

As the lowering moon winked at Davey from behind a breeze-blown leaf, he went to dreams and was a boy again in his mother's perfumed embrace.

9
October 23rd

Kevin was still amazed that things had worked out the way Sidney Weiss had promised. It had taken a bit longer than Weiss said it would—three weeks—but here he was back in his new office, waiting for his very first class to begin, with most of his books packed out of their boxes onto their shelves, and his cassette player unreeling a Brahms trio. Raymond Fillet had even come to apologize to him for what had happened—not graciously, but with enough humility to tell Kevin that college president John Groteman had, at least for the moment, put him in his place. Kevin would treasure the memory of Fillet's mock contrition.

There was another memory he would not treasure, however. Several times he had tried to call Lydia to explain his behavior. Each time she had hung up on him. He thought of going back to Eileen Connel's house, but what would he do when he got there? In Lydia's eyes, there was no redemption possible; and to Eileen Connel, adrift in her own poor, diseased mind, what could he say? She did not even know him.

Still, she knows.

Guilt assaulted him, because, he knew, he would act just as he had, given the chance again.

Was she really in love with me?

As incredible as it might be, he was willing to believe it; but again, he knew that he would only use it against her if he saw her again.

She knows, and she might remember.

The thought tortured him, but he pushed it aside.

There was only one way to redeem the guilt he felt over Eileen Connel, and that was to try to secure her place in American literature. Despite what she knew, despite the reasons for his obsession with her work, she deserved the recognition he was trying to gain her.

The class bell rang, a loud, hollow *ding!*

My God, already?

He looked at his watch, discovered that it was time to teach his first class.

Time for redemption, he thought, bringing a single book with him, held almost reverently.

They were the usual allotment of students. There were seventeen of them, freshmen, mostly arts majors with a scattering of truly interested science and engineering students, as well as the one or two business-schoolers looking for an easy grade.

Kevin entered purposefully. Someone had put a large, carved jack-o'-lantern on his desk, lit, facing him with its crooked, demonic grin.

"May I ask whom to thank for this?" Kevin said, keeping his tone light, but authoritative.

A hand went up from the back of the class.

"Nick Backman, sir." Clean-cut, sweatered, a touch of arrogance. Backman smiled. "I thought you might appreciate it."

"Well, Mr. Backman, I do. Especially—"

"May I ask a question, sir?"

"Of course, Mr. Backman."

Backman held up a copy of Eileen Connel's *Season of Witches*. "I've read this, and I just wanted to know if all that devil mumbo jumbo in it is real."

The class laughed. Kevin grinned and said, "Well, Mr. Backman, I can't say it's real, but Eileen Connel does use it for thematic effect. We'll be discussing that, shortly."

Kevin blew out the candle in the jack-o'-lantern and propped his own copy of *Season of Witches* in front of it so that it was clearly visible. He turned to the blackboard, finding a piece of white chalk.

"I'm glad some of you have already bought and read *Season of Witches* in anticipation of my arrival," he said as he sketched. "The rest of you should do so immediately. I'm sorry you were kept waiting. I understand that Mr. Steadman was discussing William Faulkner, and I promise to return to that worthy gentleman later in the semester. But for now . . ."

He finished at the blackboard, turned, and said, "What you see behind me looks as if it belongs at a football rally or a weinie roast. It's a Druidic bonfire. For my money, it should have been on the cover of *Season of Witches*. But, such is life, you see a picture of what the publisher thought, without reading the book, was inside. It's a detail of a painting lifted from the Illustrated Shakespeare Library, the three hags from the play *Macbeth*. It has nothing to do with *Season of Witches*." He turned, tapped the sketch of the bonfire with his chalk. "This, however, does.

"*Season of Witches* deals with the Celtic festival of

Saman, the Celtic Lord of Death. Each October thirty-first, the evening before the Celtic New Year, the Druids, who were Celtic priests, honored Saman by building a huge bonfire from sacred oak branches, and by sacrificing animals, crops, and probably, humans. The book concerns a young Druid, eventually sacrificed to Saman, who comes to doubt and then fight Saman's domination of the Celts.

"If you haven't figured it out by now, the festival of Saman, after some Roman and Christian tampering, eventually became what we call Halloween. And Saman became, of course—"

Nick Backman had raised his hand. "Satan?" he said eagerly.

"Correct, Mr. Backman. I see that you *have* read the book. But you must remember that in *Season of Witches,* Satan is not a supernatural being, but ultimately, a rather banal creature."

Kevin lifted the copy of *Season of Witches* from his desk, held it up. "That, in sketchiest detail, is what this book, Eileen Connel's best, is about.

"But that's not what makes it great.

"Eileen Connel is, as you have discovered if you have read this novel, a great metaphorist. For what seems on cursory examination to be a straightforward story, is, in fact, a symbol for the battle of the human soul against loss of self-identity."

Kevin pointed to the blackboard drawing. "The festival of Saman came in autumn, on the eve of winter. Winter was, for the Celts, the season of death—death of warmth, of sunlight, of crops. Days became cold, nights long, fields fallow. In *Season of Witches,* there is a concurrent bleak season of the human soul. To Eileen Connel, loss of self-identity is death. This is a recurring theme in Connel's work. Life is, to her, a search for self; and to her, the workings of the human heart and soul reflect this condition.

"To Eileen Connel's Celts, on the festival of the Lord of Death, on the eve of the Season of Death, the world is a frightening place. So, too, is the inner world. Connel's work is a triumphant attempt to illuminate search for self-identity. Her heroic young Druid priest, in his battle with Saman —who, in the end, is exposed as little more but a thief— may, ultimately, lose his life, but gains his self. I think you will find Eileen Connel an acute commentator on the human condition."

Forty minutes later, as Kevin was ending his lecture, as if by choreography, the class bell rang.

"By the way," Kevin added, amidst the rustling of papers as his students prepared to leave, "Eileen Connel has lived not ten minutes from this campus for the last fifty years. She's been nearly ignored. You and I are going to do something about that."

As his students filed out, Kevin thought, *That's redemption.*

But with a sinking heart, he realized that both his guilt, and his obsessive need to know Eileen Connel's secret, were still firmly in place.

As Kevin closed the door to his office, someone knocked on it. He opened it to find Henry Beardman.

"May I speak with you, dear boy?" Beardman said.

"Of course."

Kevin knew that Beardman was through for the day; his Monday schedule contained a single Shakespeare lecture at nine. Here, at eleven, Beardman's breath gave off the sweet-sour odor of scotch.

Beardman paused, poked a finger at the book Kevin held in his hand to better see the cover.

"My God, Shakespeare pictures on Connel," he said. "Don't these publishers have any scruples?"

"Apparently not."

Beardman walked to Kevin's desk, sat in Kevin's chair, and swiveled it so that he faced Kevin squarely. "We must talk."

"You sound like Sidney Weiss," Kevin said. "The last time I heard those words, I was nearly booted out of here."

Beardman waved a hand. "Sidney is gone," he said. "And I am here. And Raymond Fillet still wants your butt."

Is he the only one? Kevin thought, staring blankly at Beardman.

"So . . ." Beardman said, rising, placing a soft hand on Kevin's shoulder, "I want you to know I will be your ally. And, I pray, your dear friend."

"Henry—"

Beardman held up his hand, turned his head, looked away with false drama. "Oh, tell me not that I am rejected!"

"Henry," Kevin began, but when Beardman turned to look at him, the pain in his eyes was evident. Kevin was overwhelmed with pity. Beardman obviously understood what was happening to him. His power at the university, whatever it had been, was gone.

Kevin remembered the Beardman who had taught him at New Polk eight years before—flamboyant, youthfully aging, energetic, brilliant.

He softened his toneless voice and said gently, putting his own hand on Beardman's shoulder, "Henry, I'm sorry. I do want your friendship, though. . . ."

Beardman quickly recovered, put the remains of a smile on his face, waved his hand cavalierly.

"Dear boy, we can be that." He patted Kevin on the arm and left Kevin's office, closing the door behind him. Kevin heard him close the door to his own office.

Kevin went to his desk, turned the Brahms tape over in

the cassette player, and sat staring at the Shakespearean cover of Eileen Connel's *Season of Witches.*

No redemption, yet.

There was a bottle of scotch in Henry Beardman's desk, and he poured himself a drink from it. No one drank scotch anymore. No one did anything anymore. There had been a time, he thought, when he had been perfectly acceptable, perfectly current. He had rather come to terms with himself, and, if he remembered correctly, he had even been happy. He must have been nearly fifty, then. And Jeffrey had been his, too. Established, respected, known, in all ways. The village queen, but every village needed one, didn't it? Just like it needed an idiot. And he had his literature, which gave him stature. Dammit, he was good with his Bard.

The old bastard.

Maybe Shakespeare was Christopher Marlowe after all?

He laughed grimly.

There was a time when even a thought like this would have sent him into a fury of denunciation. He had seen a messianic English critic go into apoplectic fits at the mere mention of heresy in regard to Shakespeare, and for a time, Beardman's entire first lecture of each semester had been nothing more than a hellfire speech reinforcing William Shakespeare's identity, as well as the authorship of his plays.

But he had grown tired, especially after Jeffrey had died of that disease, in his arms, poor boy, begging Henry to forgive him, which he had not. Now he knew he could not get through that pulpit speech—its worn pages somewhere in the back of that drawer with the scotch—without laughing, or weeping, or possibly just going to sleep.

He used to enjoy scotch, too, a Sunday afternoon out in the Hamptons, at Jeffrey's mother's place, that beautiful deck overlooking the salted, lapping ocean, a grayish day

Jack Skrip

with mist coming, the sun very orange as it lazily sank, the Sunday papers scattered around their wicker chairs, and Jeffrey handing him a second scotch sour, just right with sugar, leaning over him, kissing his forehead gently, whispering, "Isn't this wonderful?"

Yes, it had been.

He drank again from the scotch, hated the petrol taste now, but it made him swim in memories without drowning.

"Ah, well," he said.

He capped the scotch bottle, put it back in its berth. He stood. His old Irish cap was hanging on the coatrack; he put it on, and his lined raincoat. Cold today, if he remembered. Monday. His early day. A day to play at the past. At least to try.

That Michaels boy reminded him of the past. Of Jeffrey, a little? Around the eyes, and a certain slimness to him that was similar.

"Ah, well."

He left his office. He walked slowly, purposefully, step in front of step. An old professor lost in thought. There were thoughts, all right. No one bothered him, asked to smell his breath. Thinking of Shakespeare? Turning the phrases of an old lecture to recapture their freshness? Perhaps another time.

He kept his head bowed, walked.

Off the campus, onto the main street of New Polk. A good half mile. A healthy walk, good for the circulation. *Like scotch.* He laughed a little. That was good. He was drunker than normal today, that Kevin Michaels, he thought there might have been something there, a sensitivity.

Walking. He knew where he was going. They all did, the village queens. The place was respectable enough. Some days it was even half and half now. Hetero college seniors had taken the place over in the afternoon because it was nearly empty. There had been no discouragement. That disease. Business was business.

Henry walked out of cool sunlight, the name Swan Inn scripted in white on the front of the green awning, picture of a swan on a wooden plaque next to the door, one little window with thick glass to the right.

He pushed through the oak door.

It was nearly empty. Two at the bar, in the far corner, turned face-to-face. Empty tables. My God, what time was it? He checked his watch against the clock behind the bar, a painted swan behind a plastic lens, quartz run, maybe the battery was going? Half past eleven. That Michaels boy. Usually he waited until three, had lunch, made it seem leisurely.

The bartender whose name he could never remember was on. Surly, ingrown. Bob?

"A scotch, please, Bob. Straight up. No ice." Perhaps later a sour?

As he sat, the bartender looked at him with a miffed expression. Not Bob? He thought of asking, decided not to.

The door behind him opened, light flashed in, then darkness returned. The two at the end of the bar were joined by two more—a party that moved to a table. He had a second scotch. A television was on in Bob's sight, soap operas. Shakespeare made into soda water. The same plots. Again he thought of ingrown.

He was getting very drunk. A dangerous time. He remembered now why Bob looked at him, miffed. It *was* Bob. But Bob hadn't been there long, and Peter at night knew him better. He had been in last week, hadn't he? How could he forget. After many scotches, he had asked Bob The Question. Bob had finally made him leave.

Perhaps he would leave Bob a tip.

That young man Michaels—ah well, ah well.

He was very drunk.

There was another scotch in front of him. He tasted it, found to his astonishment that it was a scotch sour. Had he ordered it? If he had, he must have passed the dangerous time. He did not remember. He tasted the sour. Good.

He looked up.

He was not at the bar. He had moved to a table, there was noise all around him. When had that happened? Had Bob moved him?

Someone returned to the table with a beer, sat down, looked into his eyes.

Oh, God.

He remembered now, the crowds coming in, the soft hand on his shoulder. When? A half hour ago? Into the back, a table in the corner where they could talk. Did he buy the first drinks? No, he had not spent any more money. He must have mentioned a scotch sour . . .

"Is your drink all right?"

Henry said, listening intently to himself speak, making sure it was really he who said the words, "Yes, of course it is. . . ."

"My name is James."

"Of course, James."

The long fingers on the hand really were touching his own hand, the eyes really looking into his own.

Didn't he know this man? Didn't he exclaim, when they had first sat down, a play he had seen years before, on television, the year Jeffrey died?

James Weston!

"My Lord," Henry said, taking the other man's hand in his own. "Please forgive me. My old mind, it jumps. Possibly I've had too much to drink. You were wonderful—or have I already said it?—in *Midsummer Night's Dream.* The PBS production. You obviously love the words, or have I already said that?"

"Say it again," Weston said. A beautiful smile, the eyes a little hooded—but of course, he was an actor. . . .

"Why are you here?" Had he asked that, too? And why was James Weston dressed in such a peculiar way? Long, stiff black trousers, suspenders, a white, stiff-looking shirt, sleeves rolled up—

"To rest," Weston said. The soft smile. Yes, he *had* already asked that question. Such patience, in such a beautiful man.

"May I . . . ?" Henry said, caressing James Weston's hand, moving his own fingers, an electric touch, over those cold fingers that needed warming. Perhaps he had asked this, also. . . .

"Would you like to go now?" James Weston said.

"Of course!"

Too quickly, he tried to rise. The afternoon a blur of noise around them, the remains of his drink on the table, James's hand rising from the table with his own in it, as if he had been asked to dance, their hands holding, guiding Henry across the floor, a blur, the blurry face of Bob, the bartender, off behind his bar, sour looking, busy, the noise pushing aside for them, excuse us, please. Out into the air.

Cold. James gently removed Henry's hand from his own, took him diplomatically by the arm. "Come, my friend." Gently, Henry tugged at his raincoat lapels to raise them around his neck.

They walked. Away from the Swan, away from the university. Henry Beardman's nearby rooms left behind, the clutter, the small, empty spaces.

"Where—?" Henry asked.

"I have a place," James answered, the faint hand of the actor on his arm, the guiding light, *What light in yonder window breaks*—

They crossed the main road. A modest steel bridge led out into the farms on their right. The land rose slightly ahead, up into the hills out of New Polk, the province of apple orchards and roadside stands.

A path. Beside a farmstand, cars angled on gravel, the smell of apples in baskets, fresh-faced people with gourds in handbaskets. To the left, off the highway, a huge pumpkin patch ranked to the foot of the hill. Customers picked among the vines, a pile of dusty fat pumpkins, mountain shaped, between farmstand and patch, small, picked rows of pumpkins beside it, toddlers squatting to lift small ones, trotting back to mother . . .

"This way," James said.

The path, thin, dusty, rock strewn, beyond the stand and field, up the soft slope of the hill. The sky overhead like a blue canvas. He used to love these days when he was younger, the dying days of the year, before sex was an issue, his childhood. His father's strong hands lifting him, his mother's close embrace under a sky like this, this end-of-year, cold harvest—

"Nearly there," James said. Henry stumbled, looking at the suddenly blurry ground. James helped him up, held his arm in a firmer embrace. The sky again, he looked up, but now it was today and he turned to see James's face.

"I could easily love you, dear boy," he said.

James smiled.

They topped the hill, a spreading plateau to the left blocked with apple trees. They descended, a farmhouse visible below.

"This is where I'm staying," James said. A nice place, tidy, recently tilled garden, clean porch, the homey creak of an opening door. Henry went in, stumbled over the sill, put his hand out to the wall to steady himself. The interior partly visible in the blur: country furniture, a stone-framed fireplace, hearth rugs over a wide-planked, clean oak floor.

"Where is the bedroom, James?" He tried to sound tender, but the words, to his regret, were slurred.

A firm hand took his arm. A guide. Kitchen ahead, small, white tiled. An abrupt left. A short hallway, pine paneling on the walls. Three doors. Bathroom on the right. A larger room straight ahead, door open, to the left another room. He stopped here. A pine bed, unmade, sheets tousled. Once a boy's room, a short line of trophies on a small desk next to the bed.

In Henry, a wellspring of tenderness rose.

"Dear boy," he said. He turned to disengage himself from the firm arm, to reach and touch the smooth cheek of the actor. But the firm arm would not let him turn. It tightened on his arm, propelled him forward.

"Ah," he said. The world became blurry again.

He felt the bed under him, a cold hand turning him over, pulling roughly at his raincoat.

"You needn't be so impatient," Henry said. "You shall have what you want."

The blurriness steadied. James Weston was astride him, face bent back away, reaching for something on the desk. Henry raised his head slightly. He saw James lift a large trophy, a football player in gold plate, arm cocked to pass.

"Dear boy," Henry said, the blurriness returning, letting his head fall back.

Something hit his face. There came a moment of disconnection. The alcohol tried to tell him that this was merely prelude, not real pain.

A second blow came, pushing the alcohol aside. As he tried to focus his eyes, a third blow closed them.

He cried out, hearing himself, and then the world closed its curtain around him, and darkness came.

10
October 23rd

Davey was awakened by the dog. He turned on his back, threw his hand out, felt it hit something. An apple. When he opened his eyes, the dog was standing over him.

"Jeez, let me sleep," he said, closing his eyes again, turning back on his side.

The dog huffed once, pushed at his back with its nose.

"All right, I'll get up." He dropped onto his back again, did a sit-up to raise himself, yawned.

"What time is it?"

The sun was well up through the trees. Late morning, maybe early afternoon. The day was chilly. Davey shivered inside his jacket, drew the wide zipper up under his chin.

"What's to eat?" he asked.

The dog huffed, sat down beside him.

Davey drew a bunch of apples close by, examined them, picked three that weren't worm-eaten, and ate them.

"What do we do for water?"

The dog huffed again, looked up at him expectantly.

He stood, brushed himself off, walked to the edge of the tree line. He looked down into the flatland below. Ben Meyer's farmhouse appeared quiet, deserted.

The dog growled behind him, continued to growl until Davey moved back into the trees.

"Fine," he said, "I know another place where we can get water."

They backed through the orchard, exiting the far side. Davey climbed the rock wall, watched the dog jump, easily clear it.

"Not bad."

They circled widely away from the Meyer orchards, cutting back toward the road. As Davey remembered, there was a path they hooked up with that brought them down near Packer's Farmstand, off Route 33. It looked as if Packer's had just opened; a few cars were parked in the gray gravel lot in front; what shelving he could see under the awning was being lined with quart baskets of apples and trays of vegetables.

"Be quiet," he said to the dog, angling toward the flat back of the building, through a picked-clean pumpkin patch. There, next to a rack of shovels and rakes, was a water spout used to clean vegetables.

In his peripheral vision to the right and behind them, someone was coming down the path from Meyer's orchard.

"Down, boy," he said. The two of them crouched flat into a rut, hidden by dry, twisted pumpkin vines.

The tall man Davey had seen the night before at Meyer's farm made his way stiffly and purposefully toward Route 33, away from the farmstand toward town.

Davey felt the dog tense beside him. He dug his splayed fingers into the dog's deep coat behind his ears.

"Easy," he whispered.

The dog began to growl, let it die out, until the tall figure had passed out of sight.

"Hell with the farmstand," Davey said. "Ben Meyer will give us water and food."

They took the path's direct route, until they soon stood on the hill, the farmhouse visible below.

Davey began to descend the hill.

The dog stayed where it was, huffing, whining in the back of its throat.

Davey said, "You saw him go into town. Come *on*."

The dog pawed at the ground, growled, refused to move.

"Stay then," Davey said. He continued down the slope.

When he got to the bottom, he looked back. The dog was trailing reluctantly behind.

Davey examined the quiet front of the house. "Mr. Meyer!" he called out.

He mounted the porch, banged loudly on the screen door.

"Mr. Meyer! Mrs. Meyer!"

He was met with silence.

He turned to the dog, who had stopped warily behind him. "What do you think? Should we check it out?"

The dog whined unhappily.

"We'll check it out."

Davey opened the screen door and went in.

He noticed the clean floor just inside the door, where he had seen the tall man working last night. The dog sniffed around it, made a mournful sound.

Davey walked back to the kitchen. Dishes were soaking in the sink; the cleanser bubbles had gone flat, leaving a grayish soapy film on top of the water. A washtowel was crumpled on the washboard next to the drying rack.

"Someone left what they were doing," Davey said.

He opened the cabinets over the kitchen counter. They were filled with plates and glasses, pots and pans. Underneath the counter was a double door. He opened it, uncovering a storehouse of food—cereals, canned peaches, cans of pork and beans. There was a bag of dog food.

"I feel bad about doing this," he said. "But I bet Ben Meyer would help us if he were here."

Under the sink was another double door, shelves with cleansers, scrub brushes, a brown grocery bag stuffed with other folded grocery bags. He drew a bag out and packed it with supplies from the other cabinet. He took from the back, moving cans and boxes forward, leaving a false line of food rowed along the front. With luck, no one would know he had been here.

He searched through the pull-out drawers above the double doors, finally locating a can opener. He searched farther back until he found another one, much older but unlikely to be missed. He threw it in the bag with the food.

"Let's go."

As they passed the door to the cellar, Davey remembered Ben Meyer's gun collection. The old man had showed it to him and Buddy once, crowing over a historical rifle.

"Hold on, boy."

Davey descended the stairs.

It was dark and musty in the basement. There was a pull chain at the bottom of the steps. Davey snapped the light on, revealing the room as he remembered it—damp, stone walled, square, an oil burner in one corner, bucket under its drip spout. There were stacks of yellowing newspapers under one mossy window, an unplugged freezer, red enameled, in the center of the floor, its top piled with boxes and a string-tied stack of *Life* magazines, John Kennedy's face on the top issue.

Against the wall directly opposite him, under its own

pull-chained light, was the well-maintained gun case, head
height, glass doors. It showed off four rifles inside, as well as
a single handgun, trigger guard hung on a peg.

Davey circled the freezer, pulled the chain in front of the
gun case. The bulb didn't light. He reached up, nearly on
tiptoe, and flicked it with his finger. It blinked, then went
out again. He turned it in its socket. It went on and stayed
on.

There was no lock on the case. Davey snapped the door
open, angled it back on its hinges. The glass rattled in its
frame.

As he studied the rifles, it occurred to him that Ben
Meyer would certainly report the theft of a missing rifle.

He closed the gun case, switched off the light. "Can't do
it."

The dog looked up at him, sniffed at the air, huffed.

"What's wrong, boy?"

The dog huffed again, cocked its head as if listening to
something Davey couldn't hear.

"Damn."

Davey snapped off the cellar light as he passed it,
bounded up the stairs, ran to the front window. Just cresting
the hill was the tall man in suspenders, helping another
man, shorter, older, wearing a raincoat and cap.

"Come on," Davey said to the dog.

He ran for the back of the house, searching for another
door. There wasn't one. He made for the short hallway off
the kitchen. Two bedrooms, a bathroom. Only the large
bedroom faced the back of the house. He tried to open the
window in it but it was painted shut.

"Shit."

He crossed to the other bedroom; through its window
Davey saw the tall man and his companion reach the bottom of the hill, approach the front yard of the house.

"Shit."

Davey ran into the kitchen, closed the cabinet doors, grabbed the bag of groceries, and hurried down the cellar steps. The dog followed. As he reached the bottom, the front door upstairs opened.

Davey crouched behind the enameled freezer, putting the bag of groceries next to him, holding the dog tightly, muzzling it against him.

"Quiet," he whispered.

The dog whimpered in the back of its throat, was silent.

Above them, voices. One of them loud, dramatic. The other gently insistent.

There were some loud steps. Davey estimated they were in the short hallway to the bedrooms.

The steps stopped over his head.

After a short interval, he heard a loud laugh, the words "You needn't be . . ." and then a muffled sound, as if furniture had been moved or bumped.

Silence.

Then, a scream.

Davey turned to ice. He heard a dull thump, another and another. The screams built to a crescendo before abruptly ending. There was a larger thump, something heavy striking the floor. He heard the sound of something being dragged, heard the front door open on its hinges. After a moment, he heard it whack closed again.

"Shit," he said. "Shit."

A shadow fell briefly across the mossy cellar window facing the front of the house. Cautiously, Davey rose and went to it. He boosted himself on one of the stacks of yellowing newspapers and looked out.

Through a filter of mossy dirt he watched the tall man drag the limp, bloody-headed body of the man in the raincoat toward the garden. The tall man left it there, went to the barn, disappeared into its open doorway.

"Jesus."

Davey jumped from the newspaper stack, ran to the gun case, yanked the door open. His hands were trembling. He fumbled a Marlin automatic out of its cradle, yanked open the ammunition drawer underneath the rack.

It was empty.

"Oh, *shit.*"

He remembered that Ben Meyer kept his ammunition upstairs in the dining room hutch. He had lectured Davey and Buddy about the stupidity of leaving everything in one place, where a fool or amateur could get their hands on it.

He heard sound outside, dropped the rifle, ran to the window, climbed.

The tall man was back with a shovel, toeing it into the dirt, digging.

Davey went back to the freezer. His hands were shaking. The dog watched him with interest, head cocked toward the window, seemingly listening.

"What are we going to do?" Davey said. He picked up the Marlin, held it uselessly in his hands. He contemplated running for the hutch upstairs, grabbing and loading a clip, facing the tall man—

The window light from outside was eclipsed. Davey's heart clutched. The tall man was standing right in front of the cellar window. Hands sweaty, Davey hugged the Marlin to his chest. He imagined the tall man's legs crouching, the tall man's face pressed against the window, his cold eyes finding Davey, the creak of the front door opening, then the slow, deliberate steps on the floorboards above, the pause, the steps slowly descending the cellar stairs—

The legs did not crouch. Davey heard the hammer of a water pipe, the rush of running water. There was the squeak of the valve closing. He saw the legs turn and retreat, saw the brief picture of a bucket, water sloshing over its side, weighing down the tall man's right hand. After a moment he heard the front door bang open, then close, heard the inner door being closed and locked.

Davey moved to the window, mounted a newspaper stack, looked out. There was no sign of the short man in the raincoat.

Upstairs, he heard the sound of a moving brush on a hard surface.

"We'll have to stay, boy," Davey said.

The dog huffed.

"We'll wait for him to leave."

In answer, the dog laid his head down over one paw, just touching Davey's jeans.

Sometime later, the brushing sound stopped. Long, slow steps traversed the house. They stopped somewhere near the living room.

After a few moments, Davey heard the tall man begin to talk. Davey thought there might be someone else in the house. But then, from the silent pauses between the tall man's words, he imagined the tall man was using the telephone.

The tall man spoke a long time. The conversation started in a low, almost mournful tone, but by the end the tall man was laughing, and then, incredibly, Davey heard him sob and distinctly say, "I know, I know." Shortly after, the conversation ended. The tall man made a second call, which went like the first.

After the phone calls, the slow steps traversed the house again. Davey put his hand on the dog's head, holding it still.

The steps stopped in front of the cellar door.

The door opened. The tall man's shadow crawled down the wall next to the steps until no light was visible from the kitchen upstairs.

Davey sat still as stone, the dog silent beside him.

The tall man's shadow crawled back up the wall. The tall man stepped back. The cellar door closed. The slow steps walked the house, then stopped, Davey estimated, around the living room.

Davey loosened his grip on the dog, rubbed behind the dog's ears. His left hand, which had gripped the Marlin like a club, loosened its hold.

Later, as darkness fell, Davey ate a can of tuna. He poured dog food out onto the floor for the dog, then made a bed of newspapers. The dog lay down next to him. There was silence from the house above.

It got chilly. The oil burner snapped on, flooding the upstairs of the house with heat, but the cellar grew damp and cold. Davey began to shiver and covered himself with more newspapers.

The dog curled close, but Davey could not banish the chills.

"Like I said," he whispered, "we'll stay until he leaves."

11
October 24th

The Time Machine, again . . .

Don't they know I hate these seminars? Yet they make me do them. Like some sort of circus freak. It *is* a show, Lydia told me that. Luckily, most of us die before we are lionized. With any luck, that will be for me, too.

Why, then, did I come? Is there still a streak of the Celtic need for confession in me, the drilling out of the soul, tickets sold to examine the cavity? We are all mock scientists. We think there must be *reasons* for everything. That is what they want to hear. *Profundity.* They want to hear we are in pain, that there are locked doors deep in the vaults of the heart, that the heart is only the blanket of the mind. (I like that, I'll put that down. Where's something to write on? Damn, this piece of paper—no, this *matchbook* cover will do.) They want to hear about the engines that drive the pen.

Tiny engines, within tiny, keyless vaults.

Kevin Michaels, the young man with the burning eyes, poor Ted Michaels's son, is the worst. A boy. Sensitive. Of course, he talked me into this, and I let him. They've come before, to sit at the feet of the master (if they saw the corns on those feet, perhaps their adulation would not be so heartfelt!) and in the process, earn their degrees. Most of them want to know *how,* what the process is. In cocktail party terms, *Where do you get your ideas?* Which makes me want to use the pen *as* the sword on them.

But Kevin Michaels is worse than his father. Relentless. Am I that much different from the rest of them, that much *surer*? Yes. Even with my failings, my hopes, dreams, I am still too much *me.* I feel comfortable in my skin, in my being, and the rest of them don't seem to have that. Danny could never stand it. It drove Bobby away; it drove Lydia into herself; it drove Eddie, poor, weak Eddie, to take himself from the world.

And it drives Kevin to me, with his burning eyes and burning heart. If only I knew! I want to tell him, to confide! Even with inner peace, there is a need to share, a need to . . . no, I won't say it.

But God help me, I've come to look forward to his visits, with his half-fawning attention to poor Lydia, his tape recorder, his notes, his interest (some of it, genuine) in my welfare and that of my family. He wants to know, because he *needs* to know, poor puppy, and I, poor dog, have . . . fallen in love with him.

There, I've said it.

Foolishness. How's that for a middle-aged writer with corns on her feet? Is it because he reminds me of my lost Bobby? Yes. And because . . . I'm in love with him. Fool . . .

What's that? Time for me to talk? I . . .

The Time Machine, the curving flight through memory . . .

Such a pretty day, my coffee getting cold, the funeral, and all I can think of is Bobby. Ten years. What would he look like now? Twenty-six years old. Would he be tall, stocky like Danny? Has he grown into an athlete? I still cry at night for him, and for Eddie, poor Eddie, gone now, and I, hope, at peace. He was not a good boy but he was mine. More Danny's than mine, but the ground has him now. The sun so orange through the whipping trees, leaves blowing into his open grave as they lowered it. The first spill of dirt. Leaves blowing in but they covered them, dying colors, it sent a chill through me. I remembered that other funeral day, so many leaves falling, the same wind blowing, and they let me watch the procession from the window. The hearses driving by, one after one, long black cars with stretched backs to hold the caskets. Such a beautiful, blowy day, a carpet of leaves unbrushed from the streets, rain the night before fastening them there, the sun breaking through into a deep, bluing sky. All those polished black hearses, the trailing parade behind. I saw Mrs. Greene crying into a handkerchief. Danny Sullivan and Ted Michaels are among them, walking together. They turn toward my house as they pass. I don't think they saw me at the window. They look so *haunted*. These pills they gave me lift me above it all, as if I'm in those breaking clouds, looking down like an angel.

Am I crying? Yes. But why do I feel so at peace?

Get away from me, Mother! Let Mr. Fields hold you!

I'm crying as they pass. I didn't need this shot. They think I'm too calm.

"She may try to follow," the doctor said. Survivor's guilt, a suicide watch. They say Ted Michaels tried to kill himself. But not me.

My coffee cold. And Eddie cold, in the ground. Poor, foolish, lost boy. Danny was there, he came, we looked at each other across the hole. No words. He didn't even try, I thank him for that. He just went home. They know he beat me, they know I threw him out. Bad wife! They still call me that in New Polk, Danny did his talking in the pubs before he left. *Free* wife.

But even Danny knew it was no good at the end, a love based on nothing, a bond based on childhood and a bad memory, words locked in an unkeyed vault, in a wife's cold heart.

They forget that it was he who sought me out for marriage, that he was drawn to me because I was the only one left. . . .

But Bobby, what would he look like? Like Danny? No, his bones were not big like that. Slender, short, like me. Perhaps like Lydia, but more of him. More substantial. Then again, maybe I'm wrong. I wonder if he ever used his love for words . . .

The Machine again. Some days the disease is so clear, the pauses between rides so sharp. Ah, the hand on the lever . . .

"Bobby. Don't leave, please. Your father, I'll make him leave you alone—"

"It's not him," Bobby says. That brooding gulf between us. "I hate it here."

"But can't you try—"

"You're drowning me!" he shouts. "Don't you see that? I just want to be alone. Away from you."

"Me?" I am genuinely shocked. He has been my favorite, even Lydia and Eddie have known this. It is something I have not been able to control. I see myself in him, my love for him is better than for the others.

When he gets sullen like this, the fire in his eyes darkens. He broods, leaves the house, walks alone for hours when his father yells at him for his lack of sports prowess, or his brother, Eddie, fights with him, or when poor, ineffective Lydia tries to console him. "You're drowning me."

And then, suddenly, I know what it is. I have been sneaking his writings away from his drawer when he is at school, and now, I know what he is going to say next.

"I'll never be as good as you."

"Bobby, you will! You'll find your own way. You love words, it's obvious—"

"Not with you smothering me."

I take him by his shoulders and draw him to me. He lets me hold him, stiffly. "Bobby, *please*. Don't you know how much I love you?"

The stiffness in his shoulders softens, then hardens again. When he speaks, his voice is soft. "I know you love me," he says. "But I have to go."

That afternoon I hear the front door close as I work upstairs. I rush to the window to see him leaving the house. When I run downstairs and open the front door, he is already down the street, his back to me, his jacket collar up, a duffel bag clutched in his right hand.

"Bobby!" I shout. "Bobby!"

He doesn't turn . . .

Into the void, the plunge through Time . . .

Kevin. I want to tell him everything today. My last chance? He will soon be gone, I know, off to Cornell for his Ph.D., and already the foolish ache of his leaving is in me. I feel so old! Forty-eight, a dinosaur, a fool. Like those talk-show women, older women with younger men, they always look so grasping, so worthy of embarrassment. He is twenty-four, *exactly half my age*. I want him to take me in his arms (fool! fool!), baggy garden pants and all, old loafers, sweatshirt, plainly attractive face, no makeup, glasses, hair needing brushing, and tell me he loves me. I would lead him to the bed. Those darkly bright eyes, oblivious, his shock of brown hair, his preoccupation, and self-absorbed smile—

What's wrong with me! He wants answers from me I cannot give. He's not in love with me, he's in love with my work and an aspect of me he wants for himself. He is consoled by my worldview—would he be comforted by my touch? No! Could he love *me*, who has periods of forgetfulness, and occasional diarrhea, who cleaned spilled food on the kitchen floor when Lydia was a baby, who smells bad in the mouth in the morning, has a sagging line of belly that never went away from Eddie's birth, and truly loved to feel her hated husband inside her, because the rough act, the moving of his lustful hands over her, made her feel loved.

Who wants to feel this boy inside her . . .

Look at how he looks at me—like a mother, a goddess—not a woman.

So, abruptly, petulantly, miserably, I try to end the interview.

And Kevin breaks down.

Suddenly, I am holding him, giving comfort. God, I wish I could give him what he wants! I wish—

Fool! There is warmth growing between us, and suddenly I am ashamed. How can I think this way! He is twenty-four, and if only he would say a word, any word—

No!

So I send him away, with his tape recorder, and his pain, out of my bedroom, out of my life—

Into Lydia's arms!

Amazingly, I hear Lydia outside my door—poor daughter who has mooned over Kevin like a schoolgirl, who has melted into my shadow—and now, suddenly, she tries to break free!

Like a voyeur, I creep to my door to see my daughter lead Kevin to her bedroom. Transfixed—Lydia's door closes! She has done what I dared not—had not the courage to do!

I walk back to my straight-backed chair and hug myself and cry.

The curse of inner peace.

If only I could give Kevin what he wants; if only . . .

The Machine, the Time Machine . . .

MY GOD, I BEGIN TO REMEMBER!

The light goes on in the backyard, through the window, and it comes back to me. The cellar window. Jerry Martin reaches out through the flames, takes hold of my wrist. Icy numbness up my arm. He tries to pull me back into the flames, but then he uses my resistance, pulls himself out of the cellar window. Blackened bits, his face falling away. I fall back, and Jerry Martin, the smell of flesh, is on top of me, his charcoaled hands clawing at my face. I feel the bones of his fingertips in my mouth.

His face comes close, hot breath, the odor of burned flesh. Nothing in his eye sockets, deep, empty wells. I scream, push against him, but he pries open my mouth, the skull-smile of his own scorched face widening, the heated air of ruined lungs.

Something small scrabbles over his tongue, hanging to the edge, dropping toward my screams and then into my mouth—

The Time Machine, the plateau, the real world, the present—

LYDIA! LYDIA! PLEASE. DEAR GOD, LET ME STAY HERE ON THIS PLATEAU, IN THIS PLACE, JUST A LITTLE WHILE. I HEAR THE WORDS, DEAR GOD, I'M BEGINNING TO REMEMBER! LYDIA! SO COLD, OH, GOD, PLEASE, KEEP ME HERE, LYDIA! LYDIA! DAMN YOU, GIRL, YOU TRIED TO TAKE HIM FROM ME. LYDIA! COME HERE, GET KEVIN MICHAELS! PLEASE! IT'S GOING, I CAN'T . . .

GET KEVIN MICHAELS!

12
October 24th

As dawn broke, there was frost around the window. Davey could see his breath. He sat up, shivering. His throat was sore. His head hurt, and there was a dull, stabbing pain behind his eyes. He felt like throwing up. He fed the dog, but could not keep any food down himself. He tried to drink the juice from a can of fruit cocktail, but the sweetness in his throat made him gag.

The morning remained cold. Davey huddled against the side of the freezer, the dog close by. He made himself a packed area of newspapers that he crawled into; the smell of yellowing newsprint made him sick to his stomach. His throat was so sore, he could barely swallow.

In the early afternoon, Davey heard the tall man stir upstairs and leave the house.

Shivering, Davey pushed himself out of his newspaper

tent and ran to the window. He climbed a newspaper bundle and looked out.

The tall man was mounting the hill away from the house. He wore no coat. Davey saw a fine film of frost on the tall grass at the foot of the hill.

The tall man ascended the hill in long strides, crested the top, was gone.

Davey waited, eye pressed close against the chilled, dirty glass, to make sure the tall man did not reappear. A surge of hope ran through him.

"He's gone!"

The dog huffed loudly.

Davey jumped from the newspapers, mounted the cellar stairs. He pushed open the cellar door, ran to the front door and out onto the porch.

He and the dog climbed the hill together.

Davey caught sight of the tall man at the bottom of the hill, heading into town.

Davey shivered with fever, but smiled at the dog and said, "Come on!"

They ran back to the house. The dog stopped by the edge of the garden and pawed at the fresh-turned soil, whining.

Davey hugged himself. "Come into the house."

The dog moved farther into the garden. His agitation grew. He ran in tight circles, growling, stopping to sit on his haunches and bark, then leaning forward to dig at the soil.

Davey watched and said, "Forget it. Come on."

The dog pawed at the ground, huffed.

Davey eyed the hill, looked at the dog.

"All right, dammit, I'll have a look."

The shovel was just inside the barn door. As he walked into the sun with it, a feverish shiver ran through him. He stopped at the spot where the dog was scratching.

He pushed the shovel in, dug quickly. Big shovelfuls of loose loam moved easily aside.

Almost immediately, he hit something solid.

"What—"

He uncovered a varicose-veined leg, the bottom fringe of a woman's skirt. Next to it was the cold, black head of a dog, the front of its face collapsed. Feeling worse than ill, Davey uncovered the body, revealing the ruined, cold face of Martha Meyer.

"Shit," Davey said. The sight, coupled with his sickness, made him vomit into the hole.

Not bearing to look, he covered the bodies with dirt.

"He killed Ben Meyer and his wife," Davey said. He looked to the dog, who barked, backed away from the garden.

"Let's get what we need and get out of here."

Davey reentered the house. He went back to the cellar, opened the gun case, withdrew the .38 handgun. He brought his supply bag upstairs.

He went through the hutch in the dining room until he found the ammunition for the .38. He loaded the gun, put the cardboard box of shells in his jacket pocket.

He retrieved the grocery bag, put the .38 in it.

"Let's go," Davey said.

He opened the front door, let the dog out. He was sweating, his mind racing, trying to think.

As he reached the foot of the hill the dog made a sound and held back.

"What is it?"

The dog ran across the yard, toward the apple orchard. Davey followed.

He turned at the first block of trees. The tall man was just topping the rise that led down to the farmhouse. With him was another man, older, huskier, almost as tall. They began their descent to the house.

"Jesus," Davey said. He fumbled in the grocery bag, tearing it. Cans and packages spilled out. He found the .38, flipped the safety off, raised the gun in the air, fired it.

"Hey!" he shouted. "Hey!"

The two men stopped, turned, located him. He waved his arms, fired the gun into the air again. "Get away!" he shouted. He put the gun down, cupped his hands around his mouth. "Get away!"

The two men stood still as statues. Then, the tall man with suspenders raised his arm and struck the other man. The other man fell to the ground. He tried to rise, but the man in suspenders struck him again and then straddled the body.

The man in suspenders searched the ground around him, lifted a rock, brought it down on the man beneath him.

Davey fired the gun again. The tall man in suspenders paused, turned to look at him. The dog barked, growled loudly, ran in circles, whined.

The tall man turned back to the man on the ground, raised the rock, brought it down. The man on the ground did not move. The man in suspenders rose, looked steadily at Davey and the dog.

"Come on." Davey thrust the gun into his jacket pocket. Abandoning the food, he ran through the orchard. He glanced back through the straight rows of trees. He saw no one. Then the tall man's form appeared, just entering the trees. When he reached the rock wall, Davey vaulted over as the dog jumped beside him.

"Run, boy."

The hill bottomed out. Davey half slid down, loosened rocks on the edge of the path tumbling down beside him.

He looked back. The tall man stood at the edge of the orchard, regarding him.

"Come on," Davey said, and he and the dog ran on.

•   •   •

He kept off the main streets, avoided places where people might know him. His fever heightened. After a while, he was shivering so badly he could hardly walk. His sight blurred, and he had to lean into the curve of a telephone or light pole, holding himself tightly, bending over, until his vision cleared and his trembling subsided.

By late afternoon, he was so weak he nearly fainted. In the park, he sat on a bench and pulled his feet up, curling into a fetal position. He closed his eyes, but immediately the world began to swim and he grew nauseous. He sat up, clasping his knees, heaving.

He said to the dog, "Only one place to go."

A half hour later, they reached it. Davey cursed to see an old green sedan, badly in need of a paint job, in the driveway.

Almost immediately, though, he was rewarded. He hid in the house's side bushes as a burly man hulked from the house, down the steps, into the car.

At first the car wouldn't start. Davey heard the man curse. But then the old sedan roared its noisy muffler, pulled down the driveway past them into the street.

The car died between reverse and drive. Once again, the man in the car cursed, tried to restart it. Davey thought he was going to get out when he finally gave up on the starter, but the man tried it once more.

The car sputtered into life and held. The transmission ground into drive and the car moved off, spitting black, oily exhaust.

Davey waited till it turned the corner, then stood up and moved to a space in the bushes. He pushed through it, onto a neglected, cracked walk, overgrown with clumps of grass, which led around to the side of the house. There was a three-step porch, a door set out of its frame, all in need of white paint.

Shivering with cold and fever, Davey held his jacket at the throat with one hand and knocked on the door.

"Come on, come on," he said.

There was darkness in the house, no sound of television or radio.

Davey knocked again, louder. "Shit, please."

He heard faint movement within.

"Come on, dammit!"

Suddenly he had to vomit. He clutched his middle, felt his head go light as helium. A sickly sweet taste filled his mouth. He struggled to fall forward, to lean against the house, but collapsed down, like a folded fan. The porch met his body. He curled over it. His head lay on the top step, a sliver of peeled paint tickling his cheek.

His stomach heaved again, throwing a trickle of bile up his throat, which he tasted and then involuntarily swallowed again.

"Jeez," he heard someone say.

He was lifted. To himself, he felt insubstantial. Racking shivers shot through his body. For a moment, he was able to bring his eyes back to the world to see the face looming over him.

He saw the face.

"Buddy . . ."

"Yeah, Davey," he heard. The word was stretched out, as if a train was pulling the words away from him like taffy. "Jeeeeeeeez . . ."

He tried to say "Yes." But a weak wash of bile rose into his throat from his constricting stomach, and his eyes were filled with heat, and the fever took him to its secret place.

13
October 24th

This is not me.

The movie in James Weston's head was out of control. In the back of his throat, he felt something constrict when he breathed, felt something like foam filling his cranium. The movies were running much too fast, edited in much too chaotic a fashion, like Fellini films. He reached his hand up and wondered if it was his own hand; he saw it from a great distance, through a telephoto lens, miles away at the end of his arm. He could barely see what the fingers were doing if he tried to wriggle them. His body below his neck felt cold, weighted, as if at the bottom of the ocean. But he knew he could run very fast if necessary, could move those hands, way out at the end of his arms, like scissor blades, if made to.

This is not me. But yes, it was. Since a time he barely

remembered, old footage of an apple orchard, a dog with a thick coat, the bite of an apple, acid but sweet—not like that acid in the back of his throat now—Ben Meyer putting his hand on his shoulder like a father, a blue, high, cold sky with blossoms of cloud, he had been in this other movie, and it was not his own. He was not the director.

But it *was* him.

He discovered this as he lay on the couch in the living room, staring at the ceiling. He felt a momentary rush of the sprocket, a letting go by the thing above the back of his throat. For a brief moment, he was really looking at the ceiling, and not just facing his eyes toward it.

He felt himself flood through his body. He held his hand up before his face, seeing it close by. A rush of memories roared through him. He gasped with the brightness of the images. He felt himself on the verge of a great revelation—

No, the thing in the back of his throat, the new director, said, immediately regaining control, putting the packing back into his cranium, starting the other movie. But the images faded slowly: Ben Meyer trying to rise as James hit him with the hoe; Martha's face as he advanced on her, the pulpy sounds of the strike, his own wheezing grunts of effort. He saw, *felt,* witnessed in CinemaScope, the joyful greed of the thing in his head, the pure electric lust, the orgasmic building toward the moment of dissolution, the climax as the curled hook of the ruined hoe shot into the eye of the dog Rags, bursting back into the brain—

He saw himself straddling an old man in an Irish cap, his own arm rising and falling, smashing a weapon into the lifeless, bloody face—

My God, what is inside me?

No.

The thing in the back of his throat pushed James Weston back deep into the recesses of himself. James realized the thing had *let* him think this last thought, had enjoyed his reaction and his full realization of his entrapment. The thing had let him free, for a tiny moment, only so that it could enjoy his despair.

Yes, the thing said, pushing him down to near invisibility.

James tried to scream, but he could no longer see through his own eyes, hear through his own ears, and knew his mouth had stayed mute.

Later, the thing let him rise into himself the tiniest bit. James felt the workings of his body far off, like a man in a tiny, windowless room in the head of a giant robot. He felt the machine heave under him, sensed the oil juice through the joints as the legs pumped and the arms swung. Before him was a movie screen before the show, a kaleidoscopic vista giving him hints of movement, sight, sound.

The screen cleared, and he saw through his eyes.

He saw, but had no control. He felt as if his head were in a clamp, his eyes taped open.

He was walking into town, just abandoning the path from Ben Meyer's orchard, past the farmstand. He saw the white, flat ribbon of sidewalk, people moving in peripheral vision as if through a fish-eye lens. He stopped for a light, then crossed the street.

He glimpsed his own long arms, at the bottom of the screen, swinging like pendulums on either side of his body. Sound came to him filtered, cottoned, fuzzy.

He crossed another street. He walked over the black tarmac of a gas station, past the pumps, caught the sharp odor of gasoline, trampled over a clump of weeds forming a boundary and onto another tarmac covered by a long fiberglass awning. The awning, supported at the far edges by white poles, fronted a glass-walled building with benches inside. Above the door, in shaded letters: NEW POLK BUS STATION.

His hearing sharpened. At the perimeter of his distorted vision, a bus yanked into view, pulled under the awning, wheezed to a stop. The long doors in the front folded open.

Passengers disembarked: an elderly woman carrying two pink hatboxes, protesting that she needed no help; an old man in a wrinkled raincoat behind her, telling her she did; a student in sunglasses, books under his arm; two men with briefcases; James's father.

His father.

In James's tiny room in the top of his head, he made a cry of astonishment. It did not reach his lips. He tried to push himself out to his extremities, to widen his eyes, throw his hands up, step back, turn. Run.

Instead, he felt his body smile, felt the muscles in his face pull back into pleasure.

"Hello, Dad," James heard his voice say. Through the faraway lenses of his eyes, he watched his father study him, aging face expressionless, holding his bag, standing at the bottom of the bus steps.

"I came," his father said flatly.

His father looked so *old.*

Now James remembered the phone call. He remembered the thing making him punch the numbers, putting anguish in his voice, pleading for reconciliation, speaking sincere words, saying he was sorry, that they had to talk, that his father must come up to meet him.

James tried to scream. But his head was held in that vise, his eyes taped open, watching through the projector lenses of his own eyes the movies directed by the thing in his throat.

His mouth said, "Thanks. All I want to do is talk. I think we owe each other at least a chance to make it right."

He saw a flicker of something in his father's eye, a crack in the stone face. He felt his smile widen. Abruptly, his father put out his hand and grabbed his arm. "Jesus, you got big. Could have played ball. You look a lot like me."

"Dad," his mouth choked out. His faraway legs stepped forward, his hands reached out, his arms enwrapped his father, held him tight.

"Never thought I was this soft," he heard his father say.

"This is the way I hoped it would be," his mouth answered, and his father mumbled something against him and held him.

James tried to scream, tried to thrash, but the movie rolled on.

They began to walk. Their long, similar strides, their rush of conversation, carried them through the gas station, across one street, another.

The sidewalk came to the grass path up the hills. James's hand took his father's arm gently. They climbed, stopped halfway up the hill for his father to rest.

"Not so young anymore, kid," he said, taking a long, slow breath, smiling. "You're in better shape than me these days."

They climbed on. His father asked him about Hollywood.

His mouth talked about cast parties, meeting Richard Burton, kissing starlets on-screen.

"Damnedest thing I ever heard. Son of mine a famous actor," his father said.

At the top of the hill they rested again. The day spread around them like a carpet, yellow fields, New Polk nestled like a pumpkin in the midst of blinding autumn colors.

"I waited too long," his father said. "I'm sorry."

"Rest, Dad."

His father looked at him evenly. "I treated you pretty tough when you were a kid. You were sixteen. I've never forgiven myself. I shouldn't have been such a hard son of a bitch."

"It was my fault, too."

His father smiled. "Can we call it even?"

"Okay."

They descended the hill.

"Tell me more about the starlets," his father said.

A gunshot sounded. James looked at his father, whose eyes widened in question. They both turned, looked at the top of the ridge by the apple orchard.

A figure was there, shouting. The dog, Rusty, was with the figure, barking.

James felt rage fill the thing in the back of his throat, almost flow out to the skin, the face.

The figure, a boy in a leather jacket, shouted, "Get away!" He held something aloft and a puff of smoke came out of it. Another echoing shot reached them a second later.

His father looked at him. "Who is that?"

His mouth answered, "No matter."

James felt his arm raise up, knock his father to the ground.

His father tried to rise. "Son—?"

James felt his hand strike his father again, push him down flat, climb over his chest, pin his arms. His hand patted the ground, came up with a weighty rock.

His father stared up at him as he hit with the rock, hit again.

See? the thing in his throat said to him.

James tried to scream, to sob, could only watch.

His legs stood him up. Through the long lenses of his eyes he looked at the boy and Rusty standing on the lip of the slope. Rusty barked. The boy's hand with the gun in it lowered. The boy turned and ran. The dog yelped angrily and then followed.

James felt the thing's rage run through him. He ran madly up the slope, long legs pumping up the dirt path, into and through the apple orchard.

He climbed a stone wall and soon reached the end of the

orchard. He felt his legs stop; saw the boy and dog retreating below, toward town.

His legs turned, brought him back into the orchard.

He stopped breathing heavily, then ran to a nearby apple tree, screaming, and began to rip the branches from the lower limbs. He squeezed apples in his fists, shouting. He bleated at the sky, throwing his head back, beat at the trunk of the tree with a torn length of branch.

Noooooooooo!

The branch broke, and he beat at the tree with his fists.

The red rage subsided.

Go, the thing in his throat said to him.

The movie darkened. Fuzziness filled James's little room. The long lenses clouded. He felt vague movement; heard the sounds of digging.

Later, the movie returned, in low light and through much fog. His eyes were staring at the ceiling in the living room of the farmhouse. There was a noise, and he felt himself rise. His legs walked stiffly to the front door and his eyes looked out, watching a black Ford Thunderbird curl up the long driveway and stop dustily in front of the house. His ears heard the driver put the car into park. Then, a door opened on either side and two people got out of the car, his agent, Samuels, and Marcie.

He opened the screen door and stepped out onto the porch; they looked up at him expectantly.

"Hi," his mouth said.

Samuels, removing his sunglasses, said, "So, big shot. You called, we came." He smiled his white smile. "Ready to be a good boy now?"

Marcie smiled, too.

The thing in his throat let him smell Marcie's hair as she

passed him into the house. His hand shook Samuels's hand warmly.

"Yes," his mouth said, so disattached from his own futile screams. "I'm ready to be a good boy now."

14
October 30th

It took Davey six days to recover.

Buddy almost called an ambulance the first night. At four in the morning, lying on Buddy's rumpled bed, Davey began talking in broken sentences, eyes wide, skin dry and hot as paper left in the sun. One hand lay limply, unknowingly, on the dog's head.

Buddy found a thermometer in the back of the top shelf of the medicine cabinet in the bathroom, shook it down, slipped the glass instrument under Davey's tongue. It read 104.2.

"Ain't good," Buddy said.

When, an hour later, Davey's temperature had climbed to 104.6, Buddy decided to call an ambulance. But just as he went to the front hallway to use the phone, headlights illuminated the living room through the front window, and he heard the bad muffler on his old man's car as it pulled into the driveway. He ran back to his bedroom and closed the door.

Davey lay quietly asleep on the pillow. When Buddy felt his forehead, he found that it had cooled.

The next day, Davey's fever dropped. By that night, he had begun to eat. Buddy stopped at the A&P after school and bought a can of chicken noodle soup, a box of crackers, a small bag of dog food. He heated the soup in a tinny saucepan on a hot plate. Davey held some of it down.

The next morning, Davey was hungrier, finishing the rest of the soup and a fistful of crackers.

After school, Buddy bought a loaf of Wonder bread and a jar of peanut butter. When the dog showed an interest in it, Davey let him lick peanut butter from his fingers.

"Sorry, I've got no money for beer," Buddy said.

"I'd just puke it up, anyway," Davey answered.

They continued like this for four more days. Buddy's father slept most of the day and went to work at six. Buddy walked the dog each night when his father left, and just before his father got home. Buddy slept on the floor, wrapped in an old quilt that shed stuffing from one end. His room was small and dirty, the bed banged up. There was a secondhand desk, covered with plastic modeling paraphernalia, Testor's paints, brushes and glue, a half-finished red '56 Corvette model, parts laid out neatly next to the box. On a pine board above the desk, supported by two cheap gray brackets, were competently finished models, including a sky-blue '58 T-bird. The walls of the room, old cracked yellow paint, were thumbtacked with old rock posters, The Doors, T-Rex, Led Zeppelin, along with Bon Jovi and Def Leppard.

On the fifth day, when Buddy got home from school, he threw his books on the floor and turned his desk chair around to face Davey. He took off his jacket, dropped it over the back of the chair, sat, leaned forward, looking at the floor, rubbing his hands. "Time to tell me what's going on."

"What do you mean?" Davey tossed aside the hot-rod magazine he had been reading. He had gotten color back into his face. The dog lay beside Davey on the bed, facing him, head resting over one paw. The dog made a deep, contented sound in his throat as Davey dug his fingers deep into the dog's coat, behind the ears.

"Don't give me any bullshit, man. You were talking like crazy when you had that fever. Something about a guy killing another guy. *Lots* of guys."

Davey looked at him, said nothing.

"Come *on*, Davey! You said some guy murdered Ben Meyer and his wife, buried them somewhere."

Davey continued his even stare. "I must have been dreaming."

Buddy sat up, hit his knee with his fist. "You dream that .38 in your jacket pocket? God*dammit*, Davey, you don't trust me? You think I'm a jerk like everybody else does?"

"Forget the whole thing, Buddy."

"Look at you! You're scared shitless! I've never seen you like this before."

"I said forget it. Thanks for the help. You're not a jerk. Believe me—"

Buddy's face reddened. He stood up. "I'm not a jerk, but you can't trust me, right? Good enough to use, but not good enough to let in on the secret, right?"

"Hey, calm down, you'll wake your old man up."

Buddy's face flushed with anger. "Who cares!" he said. "Fuck everything! My old man thinks I'm no good for anything. Nobody thinks I'm good for anything. The college boys give me a hard time, I'm supposed to take it—"

"Nick Backman still bothering you?"

Buddy's anger softened to embarrassment. "He said you were chickenshit for running away from home, so I challenged him to fight."

"Buddy—"

"I don't need you this time, Davey. Nobody fights for me anymore. This time I take Backman alone."

"Where?"

"His house, tonight. His parents won't be home. He promised, just me and him. No funny business this time."

"You can't trust him."

"Can I trust *you*?" Buddy's anger grew. "Know what I'm gonna do? I'm going up to Ben Meyer's place, check it out myself." He stood, pulled his jacket off the back of the chair, put it on, zipped it up. "From now on, I do everything myself." He walked to the door, kicked his schoolbooks aside, yanked the door open.

"You can't do that," Davey said from the bed.

Buddy stuck his chin out defiantly. "Why not?"

"Because you'll get killed."

"Bullshit."

"There's a guy in Ben Meyer's house that's murdered everybody he's met—"

"Too late, Davey. I'm going, no matter what."

Davey studied Buddy's set face. "Don't."

Buddy reached for the door.

"All right," Davey said, getting up from the bed.

Buddy stopped. "What?"

"I'll go with you. As soon as your old man leaves for work. I owe you that. And then I'll go with you to Nick Backman's."

Buddy flashed his white smile. "All *right*."

In the few days Davey had been in bed it had gotten colder, rawer. The sun was lower, a deeper orange; the trees whipped a little tighter in the cutting wind. Fallen leaves blanketed the streets, lined the gutters, were sent billowing by passing cars. The houses wore lines of leaves in their gutters, along their foundations. Carpets of leaves covered browning front lawns. Piles of them, raked next to walkways, were peeled by the wind. There was, everywhere, an odor of dried leaves.

And, in those few days, the houses of New Polk had readied for Halloween. Newspaper-stuffed scarecrows with pumpkin heads, and stuffed black witches with brooms and peaked charcoal hats above long faces, guarded porches. Windowpanes were crowded with jointed skeletons, white bones bent into dancing position, smiling skulls making them look vaudevillian. Every porch and stoop held a pumpkin—fat, bursting at the seams, ripe, dark orange, uncarved. There were autumn baskets of gourds: fat and hard, green, deep yellow. One picture window had a jointed cardboard banner that said in big, shaky white letters, BOO!

Buddy did his bopping stride; Davey walked with his head tucked into the collar of his jacket, like a turtle. A police cruiser crossed their path a block ahead. They ducked away, as if from a cold wind, until it went on.

"Fucking cops," Buddy said.

As they turned off the walk to the dirt path near Packer's Farmstand, Davey dug his fingers deep into his pocket, wrapped them around the .38.

They circled around through the orchard. After climbing the rock wall, they made their way into the tree blocks.

Neglected apples lay rotting on the ground. The orchard was permeated by the sugary odor of decay.

They stopped when they saw the lights of the farmhouse rise into view below.

A car was parked out front, a shovel resting against its hood.

"That's a brand-new T-bird," Buddy said.

"Great. Seen enough?" Davey asked.

"Are you kidding?" Buddy laughed, began to walk down the hillside.

Davey reached out, held him. "Let's leave."

The defiant look had not left Buddy's face. "I told you, I'm not taking any more shit from anybody. The only way I go is to see."

"If that's what you want. But let's see if anyone's home first." Davey reached beneath his jacket and pulled the .38 out. He raised the gun and fired one shot. It popped loudly, echoed, died.

No one came from the house.

"Okay," Davey said. "But be ready to run."

He quickly descended the hill, holding the gun in front of him.

Buddy followed.

The dog stayed by the tree line, making an angry sound in his throat.

At the bottom of the hill, Davey crossed the yard and walked straight to the shovel leaning against the hood of the car. He pulled it from its resting place, handed it to Buddy, pointed at a freshly tilled spot near the edge of the garden. "Dig."

Buddy dug, struck something solid. He uncovered a man's hand, stiff and white as marble, the sleeve of an expensive-looking suit.

"Jesus," Buddy said.

"Had enough?"

Buddy moved over a few feet, dug in another fresh spot until he uncovered the blood-clotted top of a boy's head. The face fell back, revealed an open mouth filled with a spill of soil.

"This is no fucking joke."

"I told you," Davey said.

"Yeah." Buddy dropped the shovel, turned to vomit.

With the side of his sneaker, he pushed dirt back over the boy's face.

"Ben Meyer and his wife are in there," Davey said. "So's their dog. There's also a guy in a raincoat from town. It's been almost a week since I was here. Who the hell knows how many others there are."

"All right, Davey, we can go—"

At the top of the hill, the dog howled.

The screen door on the house banged open.

"Oh, Christ."

Davey went cold. He turned to see the tall man in suspenders step out onto the porch. His face was blank, white as the moon. His hands hung at his sides listlessly. He turned from Davey to Buddy.

"Run!" Davey shouted.

They ran.

The tall man loped after them.

Davey and Buddy hit the hill hard. They were halfway up when the tall man began to climb. By the time they topped the hill, the distance between them was only thirty feet.

"Move it!" Davey shouted.

Buddy started to go down. He slipped on a row of stones, recovered. The dog barked, ran back. Buddy regained his footing and kept running.

Davey retraced his old steps through the blocks of apple trees toward the stone wall. He glanced back. The tall man was closing the gap, arms working like pistons at his sides, long legs churning.

"Buddy, the wall!" Davey yelled. "Jump it!"

The wall came quick. Davey hurtled it, catching his back sneaker on the very top. He tumbled over, hit, dropped the .38. He jumped to his feet as the dog and Buddy leaped simultaneously.

Buddy hit the wall awkwardly. He set his foot halfway up

the rock face and started to hoist himself up and over. The tall man reached out, caught the cuff of Buddy's jeans, closing his hand around his sneaker.

Buddy's momentum carried him over the wall, dangling in the tall man's grip.

"Help me!" Buddy shouted.

Davey searched the ground frantically for the .38. He found it. As he stood up, the dog leaped, howling, and caught the tall man's wrist in his teeth. He held, twisting, until the tall man roared and let go of Buddy's ankle. The tall man raised his other hand to strike as the dog let go.

"Go!" Buddy shouted. He scrambled to his feet and followed with the dog.

The tall man stood at the wall and began to climb it. By the time he had made it awkwardly over, Buddy and Davey were fifty yards down the slope of the hill.

"Keep going!" Davey said.

"Jesus," Buddy gasped, "his . . . hand on me . . . was . . . like . . . ice."

When they reached the dirt path to the main road, they stopped.

Behind them, in the dusk, there was no sign of the man in suspenders.

Davey tucked the .38 into his belt. "Now what do you think?"

"I think," Buddy said, resuming his bopping stride, "as soon as I fight Nick Backman, we get him to call the cops for us."

On Nick Backman's block, porch lights were on. But they were restricted beacons, brightening their spot of night, leaving the rest of the world black. A single streetlight was on, its long pole settled at an angle by the root push of a nearby oak.

Two houses from Backman's, in front of a darkened Cape Cod, Buddy halted. "I want you to stay here, Davey," he said.

"Are you crazy?"

"Listen," Buddy said. "Backman hates your guts. If you show up, he won't help us get this guy at the Meyer place. After he punches me out, he'll definitely help."

"You're going to let him beat up on you?"

Buddy grinned in the darkness. "Shit, we both know I don't have a chance against him anyway."

Davey said, "I don't like it."

"It's the only way. You know the cops won't believe us without Backman's help. He's a shithead, but he's respectable. You stay here, keep an eye out. I might be in there awhile. If the tall bastard shows up, use your .38 on him."

"I still don't like it."

"There's no other way, Davey boy."

Davey hesitated, then said, "Okay."

Buddy thrust his hands into his pockets, went into his bopping walk away from Davey. Suddenly he stopped, strode back.

"Mind if I take the mutt?" he said.

Davey looked at the dog.

"For companionship," Buddy said. "In case Backman tries anything. Maybe Nick won't beat up on me so bad if I have the dog with me."

Again, Davey hesitated. "All right."

"Thanks." Buddy turned to the dog. "Come on, pooch."

"Go on," Davey said quietly.

The dog went with Buddy. As they walked away, the dog glanced back, and Davey waved at him to continue.

Buddy and the dog made the turn into Nick Backman's driveway. Davey, feeling suddenly very alone, holding the .38 like a talisman, leaned into the darkness to wait.

. . .

As he had promised, Backman had left the sliding glass door in the backyard open. Before going in, Buddy glanced at the cellar window. It was a dark rectangle, no light on.

The dog followed him into the house.

"Scalizi!" Backman greeted him. He was sitting on the long couch in the family room, TV remote in his hand. The big-screen television was on. A bowl of popcorn sat on the coffee table in front of him. Nick wore a blue oxford-cloth shirt, clean chinos, leather slippers. He rose to shake Buddy's hand. "Ready to have your tail whipped?"

"Sure, Nick," Buddy said.

"Good." Backman smiled. He looked at the dog. "This your corner man?"

When Backman reached down, the dog moved his head aside, giving a warning sound.

Backman straightened. "Touchy. Want a soda? Beer?"

"A beer, yeah," Buddy said.

"Great." Backman walked to the cellar door, opened it. "By the way, any sign of that asshole friend of yours?"

"Davey?"

"That's the man."

"Nothing," Buddy said.

"I hear they're thinking of going national with it." Nick laughed. "Can you see Putnam's face on a milk carton?"

"Sure."

Backman snapped on the cellar light. "Beer's downstairs," he said casually. He took a step down, stopped, looked back. "Coming?"

"No jokes this time, Nick?"

Backman laughed. "My *Lord,* no. That's all over with. It's just you and me tonight. You know, I like you. You're not like that jerk friend of yours. Come on, we'll talk, have a drink, maybe play a little billiards, then we'll have our little fight. *Mano a mano.*" Backman laughed. "Maybe we'll just get drunk, forget about the whole thing. Okay?"

"Sure, Nick. Listen—"

Backman held up his hand. "Drinks first, Buddy. All right?"

"Yeah."

"Good." Backman turned his back on Buddy and descended the cellar stairs.

Buddy and the dog followed. Ahead, Backman snapped on lights. A long bank of neons blinked on; the hanging Tiffany lamp flared whitely over the pool table. It was littered with unracked balls. Backman strolled to the bar against the back wall of the cellar, angled behind it, opened a small refrigerator, and pulled out a beer bottle. He poured the beer carefully into a glass. He returned, smiled, handed Buddy his beer, racked the balls. Backman chose two cue sticks, handed one to Buddy.

"There's chalk if you want it."

"That's okay, Nick—"

"Beer okay?"

"Sure. Look, there's something—"

Backman prepared to break, straightened, looked at the dog.

"Okay if we put the mutt in the toolroom for a little while? If my parents come home and find a dog in the house . . ." He made a cutting motion across his throat with his index finger.

Buddy suddenly felt warm. He unzipped and peeled his jacket off, laid it on the billiard table. "I don't know . . ."

"Come on," Nick said reasonably. "Like I said, they'd kill me."

"Well, okay . . ."

Buddy helped Nick lead the dog to the toolroom. Nick turned on the light, waited for Buddy to retreat, pulled the door closed. The dog began to whine.

"Howl all you want," Backman said cheerfully.

Buddy still felt warm. He felt achy in the joints, light-headed.

"Hey, Nick—"

"Don't worry, Scalizi." Backman laughed. "You won't die. Just a pinch of something in your beer."

"The dog—"

"The dog can bark all he wants. It's a well-built house. Nobody will hear him."

"Wha—" Buddy said. His head was badly fogging. His legs and arms felt weighted. He sat down on the floor, held his head up with effort, tried to look at Backman. "What . . . are you doing?"

Backman laughed. "Like I promised, no more jokes." Backman's face grew larger through the fog. Buddy felt Nick's hand fall heavily on his shoulder.

"But . . ." Buddy said, "we need your help . . ."

Backman laughed, loud. "Sure, Scalizi. Anything you say."

In a moving rush, Buddy came back to consciousness. He was in darkness. He heard the dog whining, scratching at the wood of the toolroom door.

He was on his back. He tried to lift his hand but discovered it was bound. He couldn't rise. He felt air move over him. He angled his fingers inward toward his body, felt the elastic top of his underpants, nothing above or below them. He turned his palm downward, touched a smooth, cottony surface.

A light went on behind his head.

Buddy twisted his head around, saw a yellow glow descending the cellar stairs. A candle. He saw the hand holding it, an arm, a face. Backman, naked to the waist, face painted with reddish streaks.

Behind Backman, in near shadow, came Andrea Carlson and Brenda Valachio. They were in panties and bras. Andrea held Nick by the shoulder for guidance; Brenda clutched Andrea, giggling.

"Be quiet," Backman said solemnly.

Buddy realized that he was bound to the top of the billiard table.

When he reached the bottom of the cellar steps, Backman walked slowly toward Buddy. He placed the candle, set in a dish, near Buddy's head.

"What are you doing, Nick?" Buddy said. He could feel the candle's heat.

"Quiet."

The girls bent over Buddy. Andrea held up something that looked like a thick pen. She took off its cap, turned up the squat point of reddish lipstick. She stared gravely into Buddy's eyes.

"Go on," Backman said.

Brenda Valachio broke into laughter.

"Shut up," Backman said.

Brenda continued to laugh. "I can't help it, Nick."

Buddy heard a loud slap. He turned his head to see Brenda Valachio holding her cheek, staring wide-eyed at Backman. "You *bastard.*"

"Shut your mouth, Brenda," Andrea Carlson said.

Brenda faced the two of them angrily, then caved in. "All right," she said petulantly. "As long as there's more coke later."

Andrea turned to Buddy. "This won't hurt," she said gently. She dug the point of the lipstick into Buddy's cheek. He twisted his head aside.

"Hold him, Nick," Andrea said.

Buddy looked back to see Nick Backman's face, staring down at him, upside down. There were long streaks of lipstick like war paint down his cheeks, across his forehead.

Nick clamped Buddy's head between his palms. "Just be still," he said.

"This isn't funny," Buddy said.

"It's not a joke," Andrea said. She met Nick's eyes. He nodded.

She dug long streaks of red onto Buddy's face.

"Now his body," Nick said.

She ran the lipstick over Buddy's chin, down his neck to his chest. She made two large circles around his nipples, drew an arrow on his belly, pointing downward.

"Now the rest," Nick said.

Buddy felt Andrea's fingers slide beneath the elastic on his underpants, pulling them down.

"Hey, listen," Brenda said. "I mean, this could get heavy. I mean, do you think you should . . ."

"For the last time, shut up, Brenda," Nick said. "I don't want to have to tell you again."

"Well . . ."

"Finish up, Andrea," Backman said.

"Leave me the fuck alone!" Buddy shouted. He tried to kick his bonds loose.

Nick said, "Buddy, just be quiet."

"No way! Let me go, Nick!"

"Would you like me to kill the dog in front of you? I'll do it if I have to."

"You wouldn't do that."

"Yes, I would."

Buddy thrashed; he felt Nick's palms clamp on his head once more.

"Make it fast," Nick said.

Andrea pulled Buddy's underpants over his thighs, drew two deft circles on the sides of his buttocks, pulled the underpants back up.

"That wasn't so bad, was it?" Nick said.

Buddy stopped thrashing. "That's it? You'll let me go?"

Nick turned to look at Brenda, who sat cross-legged on the floor, head in her hands. "Brenda," he said, "we need you now."

"No, I don't think so," she said weakly.

"You're in it all the way, Brenda."

She raised her head, looked at him. "No, Nick. I can't."

Backman smiled. "You want a little snort first?"

Her face brightened. "Could I?"

"Go get it. Get the rest of the stuff, too."

She got to her feet, ran up the stairs, returned momentarily with a paper shopping bag.

"Cut it on the coffee table," Nick said.

Brenda removed a Baggie from the shopping bag, flaked cocaine from it, cut it into thin lines with a razor, reached back into the bag, produced a tiny cocktail straw.

"You first," Nick said.

Brenda pulled two lines of coke greedily into her nose. She handed the straw to Nick, who passed it to Andrea. Nick cleaned up, snorting what was left, then put everything back into the bag.

"Feel better now, Brenda?" he asked.

She nodded, looked evenly at Buddy. "Sure, Nick. I'm okay."

"Good."

Buddy said, "Nick, let me go."

"Can't do that, Scalizi. We took an oath."

"What oath?" Buddy's voice cracked.

Nick said nothing. They heard the dog's desperate scratching behind the toolroom door.

Nick reached into the paper shopping bag, drew out a black-handled carving knife with a long, thick, sharp-looking blade. He reached in again, brought out a frayed paperback.

Buddy laughed uneasily. "That book again? This *is* a joke, right?"

"No joke," Nick said.

Andrea and Brenda positioned themselves to either side of the billiard table, near Buddy's head. Backman, holding knife and book, climbed up onto the foot of the table and knelt, moving forward on his knees until he rode Buddy's midsection. He straightened his back, his head nearly touching the Tiffany fixture.

"Sorry, Scalizi," he said, "but someone had to be sacrificed."

"What are you doing!" Buddy screamed. He yanked desperately at his bonds, tried to raise his hands off the table.

"Say the words," Nick said, handing the book to Andrea.

Andrea found a marked spot in the paperback. "Saman, great Lord of the Dead, take this offering. We honor you this day, all days, and pray you grant us the continuance of life immortal. For in you, death is life."

Backman brought the knife high until it bumped the Tiffany fixture. Light rocked nightmarishly across Buddy's eyes. He saw Nick Backman lower the knife toward his heart—

"No!" Buddy screamed.

The knife, tight in Backman's clamped hands, froze inches from Buddy's chest. Nick moved his hands aside, dropped the knife, and rolled from the table, laughing helplessly.

Brenda and Andrea collapsed, howling with laughter.

"Christ, you are *stupid,* Scalizi!" Backman howled. "Twice you fall for the same gag. Jesus!"

"Goddammit, Nick!" Buddy wailed. "Goddammit, you scared the shit out of me!"

Backman couldn't stop laughing. "It was all an act, Scalizi."

"But you hit Brenda—"

Brenda rolled onto the floor, giggling.

"Let's show him," Nick said.

Still laughing, Brenda sat up and slapped her thigh as Backman pretended to hit her.

"Understand?" Nick said. "A joke. I just couldn't resist seeing how stupid you are."

"And now we know," Andrea said.

Grinning, Backman reached out to Andrea, kissed her, put his hand to her bra-covered breast, lowered her to the floor.

"That's right, Buddy," Brenda said, getting up, laughing, approaching the billiard table. She picked up the carving knife, made a grotesque face, held the knife over Buddy. In a deep, falsely solemn voice she said, "You must be sacrificed—"

A large hand slipped over hers. It clamped over the handle of the carving knife, pried it from her fingers. "Let me."

"Hey—" Brenda said. She twisted away, looked with surprise at a tall man with a pale face, dressed in white shirt and suspenders.

"Oh, God," Buddy said.

"Who—" Nick Backman began. He rose from the floor as the stranger slashed out with the knife, cutting a clean line through Brenda Valachio's neck under the chin.

Brenda staggered back. Her gasp was cut short as a floodline of blood burst from her severed jugular.

"Jesus!" Nick Backman cried. The tall stranger faced him. Nick moved back toward the bar.

Andrea Carlson made a dash for the cellar steps. The tall man kicked at her feet, tripped her to the ground, drove the knife deep across the back of her neck. Her head dropped forward in a gurgling scream as blood poured across her back.

"Jesus God! Somebody help me!" Nick said. He backed up until he hit the edge of the bar. He started to slide to one side. The tall man held his arms wide as he advanced, compensating, restricting Backman's movements.

Crying, Nick fumbled behind the bar, producing a highball glass. He brought it down on the bar top, but as the brittle glass broke, it cut his hand across the palm. He dropped the weapon.

"Davey!" Buddy screamed. *"Davey!"*

The tall man closed in on Backman. Nick pushed himself up onto the bar, managed to swing his legs over the back.

The tall man lunged, threw himself across the top, and stretched his long arms over, catching Backman by the hair.

Thrashing at his ropes, trembling with cold terror, Buddy twisted his head to see the tall man holding Nick Backman's head up, while his other hand drove the knife across in short, savage half-circles. Nick gave an unearthly scream. There was a liquid ripping sound. The tall man straightened, holding Nick Backman's severed head, the open mouth dripping blood. It landed sideways on the bar where he dropped it.

The tall man approached Buddy, his face a stony mask.

"Jesus, no!"

The tall man stabbed viciously down with the knife. Buddy felt a burst of hot pain in his leg above the knee. The tall man turned the knife, wrenched it out, raised it to stab again.

There was a howling from the locked toolroom, a desperate scratching sound against the door.

The tall man straightened. The mouth split in a thin, almost lipless smile. The hooded eyes looked like those in a jack-o'-lantern. "Rusty?"

The tall man walked to the toolroom door. He raised his foot, kicked the door.

The door flew open. The tall man stood waiting, nearly filling the dark doorway.

"Rusty?" His voice was filled with hollow affection. "Come on out, boy." He stepped into the room.

Whimpering with cold, fright, and frustration, Buddy

pulled against his ropes. As if by magic, the bond holding his right wrist gave way. He sat halfway up on the billiard table, yanking at the rope on his other wrist, working it loose.

In the toolroom, the dog growled. Buddy heard the tall man curse loudly.

The knot on Buddy's left wrist gave way, unraveled, fell aside.

"Here, Rusty!" the tall man shouted.

Buddy's trembling hands worked at the rope around his left ankle. He struck the deep wound in his leg accidentally, cried out.

The tall man stood looking at him from the toolroom doorway.

Buddy pulled the rope from one ankle, then the other. He tumbled off the table. When he tried to stand, his wounded leg collapsed. He pulled himself up, using the billiard table for support, and, crying in pain, launched himself toward the stairway.

As the tall man stepped forward to block Buddy, the dog attacked, hitting the tall man on the right side, closing over the hand holding the knife.

Buddy hobbled to the stairs, fell, boosted himself up, and began to climb.

The tall man jerked his hand up and threw the dog off. The dog yelped, moved back, avoiding the tall man's knife thrust.

Buddy was halfway up the stairs. With each step, a bolt of agony fired through his leg.

The tall man stumbled toward the stairs. Once more, the dog attacked. The tall man sheltered his right hand so the dog could only bite at him below the shoulder.

The tall man reached the bottom step, started to climb.

"Little bit more," Buddy begged, fighting the agony in his leg. "Little—"

The tall man's hand gripped his leg, crawled up it, found the open wound, dug into it.

Buddy's eyes went white with pain.

"Davey!"

The tall man raised his knife hand, hammered it down into Buddy's back.

"Davey . . ."

Buddy heard the dog fighting, ripping at the tall man.

"Too late, boy . . ."

Through the descending curtain, Buddy looked up. The top step was only inches from his face. He saw the dog vault overhead to the top of the stairs, felt the tall man scramble over him, screaming rage, stepping on Buddy's ruined back.

"Davey . . ." Buddy breathed.

Davey had waited forty minutes in the shadows when the dog appeared, running like a greyhound from Nick Backman's house. The dog jumped at him, grabbed his sleeve with its teeth, tried to push him off the sidewalk.

"Hey—"

The dog kept pulling at him, growling.

"All right, all right."

He backed across the darkened front lawn of the nearby Cape Cod, stopped in a deep pool of shadow near the side. There was a lawn chair there, a Halloween figure sitting in it, newspaper-stuffed clothes, plastic pumpkin for a head.

"Where's Buddy?" Davey said.

The dog eyed the street intently.

Suddenly, the dog tensed.

Davey caught sight of something: a tall, dark shape among the street shadows, moving silently by.

Davey's heart went numb as the tall man in suspenders, his white shirt drenched red in blood, entered the illuminated cone of the single streetlight.

As the tall man passed silently on, Davey bent, held the dog's head.

"Where's Buddy?"

The dog huffed hoarsely, tried to nose Davey back into darkness.

"I've got to see what happened to him."

The dog whined, then followed.

Davey moved across front lawns until he reached Nick Backman's house. He went quietly to the back. The sliding door was open. He pushed past the curtains, walked to the cellar door in the kitchen, looked down.

"Oh, shit," he said. He stared down at the reaching, silent body of Buddy Scalizi. Davey touched the black handle of the knife in Buddy's back, tried to pull it out.

The coppery smell of blood rose from the cellar like stomach-churning perfume.

The dog barked in protest as Davey descended the cellar steps. Davey's eyes, his nose, registered blood. There were bodies everywhere. The dog, at the bottom of the stairs, whined.

In a daze, Davey saw a paper bag, reached into it, lifted out a plastic Baggie filled with what looked like cocaine.

"My God, boy—"

"Don't move," a voice said behind him. Davey heard sirens. He looked up to see Officer Johnston's .38 police special aimed at him. The officer advanced, lifted Davey's jacket, yanked Davey's .38 out of his belt.

"Run, boy!" Davey shouted, and the dog mounted the stairs and ran off.

"On the floor," Johnston's hard voice said. The cop pushed Davey flat on his stomach, yanked his hands around his back, cuffed him.

"Oh, good Christ," another cop said, moving down into the cellar. "There was a dog—"

"Fuck the dog," Johnston said. To Davey, he said, "Get up."

Davey began to cry. He felt a blow across his face. He looked up into the angry face of Officer Johnston and said, "I know who did this."

Johnston hit him again. "So do I, fucker."

Davey wanted to cry again, to be five years old with his tiny hand lost in his mother's. But that real world was truly gone now, and he knew, suddenly, that he had grown up.

"I know who did this," he repeated.

The cop kicked him. "Keep your mouth shut."

Later, after Officer Johnston had hit him again, when they were putting him in the patrol car, with the ring of sleepy, curious, bathrobed neighbors staring in at him, Davey thought about the dog, and smiled.

BOOK THREE

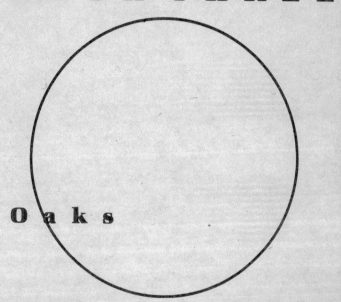

Oaks

15
October 31st

There was blood on his shirt, but it didn't matter. It was Halloween, his day, and no one would notice.

There had been plenty of times, before the soaps and TV movies, when James Weston had done his own makeup. If it had been necessary, he would have brought enough of Weston up to do it.

But there was no need.

He brought Weston up to let him see the house, to let him know what was going to happen. To hear him scream.

Quiet, he said, and James Weston stopped screaming, continued to see.

Watch.

He knocked on the door.

A girl answered. Thin. Sad faced.

"I'm looking for your mother," he made Weston say pleasantly.

"I'm sorry, she's not here."

He smiled. "Don't you recognize me?"

The girl studied him. "I'm sorry. No."

He told her who he was.

She cried and held him and made him come in. She made tea. For an hour, he listened to her, let James Weston, anguished, helpless, listen to her talk about her mother, herself, her sad attempt to love a man she despised named Kevin Michaels.

She was very sad, and wan, and thin.

Then she told him where her mother was, and he killed her.

White walls.

Were these the walls of her office? No. White walls. Where . . . ?

Lydia? Was Lydia here, in those walls, perhaps, pressed into them like a dried flower? Pale, indistinct . . .

"Lydia! Tell your father dinner is ready!" she called.

But Lydia wasn't here. Lydia was home, in the empty house, and she was . . .

Yes. A memory. The ride in the ambulance. Dr. Carpenter's face, so long and earnest. She wished she had her legal pad, her pencil now, to describe his face. She imagined he had been thinking more about his dinner than her.

"Nurse!" she cried. But no one came. There had been a visit earlier in the day: a white uniform, the flat smell of stiff starch. A bland face looking into her eyes, rough hands under her body, tucking, pushing sheets, a flat hand on her back (the Time Machine? No), propping her up like a doll, knocking pillows into shape. The sound: *whump whump,* little puffs of air on the back of her neck. She felt light as a pillow feather, frightened.

Lydia?

"Lydia, tell your father . . . !"

The witch, *The Wizard of Oz.* Lydia hid her eyes when the monkey men stole Dorothy into the air. The boys liked it. Almost Easter, on television every year. It was on so many times, Lydia hid her eyes . . .

"Tell your father!" she shouted.

The walls.

Scrubbed white. The smell of disinfectant in the corners. They should have water-mopped it out. She hated white. The dirtiest color. The illusion of cleanliness.

The door opened, old oak painted white, three panels. A face looked in.

"Are you all right, Mrs. Connel?"

Witch's mask.

The Wizard of Oz? No.

Starched white uniform. The nurse lifted the mask. Halloween. Blank face. "Did you call?"

"Lydia?" she said.

The nurse shook her head, retreated. The sound of a party, the nurses' station, someone laughing. Halloween. *Har har.* An unpleasant sound.

I observe, Mrs. Greene, I observe!

The funeral procession going by the house, her face at the window, pushing at the pane with the flats of her hands, feeling as if she must float through and over the heads of these living like an angel. . . .

Lay me down with lillies, she wrote in her secret diary. The first doctor read it; he said he didn't but she saw him take it when she was supposed to be asleep. Pills. Her mother and Mr. Fields talking to the doctor. He took the diary out of his white coat pocket. Where is Father? Is Columbus, Ohio, far away? He won't come, her mother said, lips tight. Take your pill, to sleep. Mr. Fields pretended to study the walls.

Lay me down with lillies, the fields of night my blanket bright . . .

The black caissons, her hands on the flat, lucid panes, sadness only. Peace. If she told the doctor that she was changed, that it was only a poem about peace, would he believe her?

No.

What happened to me? Why do I know these things . . .

The cold up her arm . . .

Halloween.

That ugly laugh, *har . . .*

Jerry Martin.

"Hello."

Three white panels—no. Someone was there in the doorway. Not the Halloween nurse. She was on the plateau. *Stay.* Tall, nearly up to the doorframe, pale as the white walls. *Dirty color.* Thin, suspenders, white shirt covered in bleached red.

The face . . .

"Hello, Mother."

"My God. Bobby."

She said it, knew it. It was him. Danny's height, taller, her slimness. Lydia, in the face. So pale . . .

"Where . . ." she said.

"In California, Mother. An actor. I changed my name, just like you. James Weston. Maybe you've seen me." He smiled, a slight, straight thing.

Why did it look false?

"I didn't know . . ."

"Did you miss me?"

"Oh, Bobby." She held her hands out, fingers splayed. She wanted, very much, for him to come to her.

He walked to the foot of the bed, stopped. The odd smile.

"You don't recognize me? An actor, not a writer. But I use words."

"Of course, Bobby." The fingers reached, wanting his touch.

He edged around the bed, held his hand out.

Her fingers strained, met his. She took his hand and he gripped her wrist, a vise hold.

Numbness.

Ice cold, up her arm.

"Oh . . ."

"It's me." He smiled at her, Bobby's face—

She remembered the rest.

—and into her mouth. She feels it scrabbling up into the back of her throat. A burst of images, the burning of a huge bonfire, oaks—

"No!" she screams, turns her head aside, gagging. The thing falls. She feels it strike her teeth and she opens her mouth wide, gagging, pushing with her tongue, and the thing drops free.

As it falls, scrabbling at the ground, churning its tiny legs down away from her, she feels, like a rifle shot of truth, an overwhelming—

"I remember!" She looked up at the face of her son. "I remember!"

"Yes," he said.

"I'm not afraid," she said. Her face was radiant. "You can't hurt me."

"You're alive. I already have." He loomed over her, his mouth opening. "You wrote about me."

"Yes."

"I want to hurt you, but I want you to live to die the way you were supposed to." His hands, her son's hands, descended upon her. "Let me tell you what I've done, and what I'm going to do. . . ."

16
October 31st

When a sharp, loud, impatient knock came on Kevin's office door, he knew immediately who it was.

"Come in."

The door opened. Raymond Fillet turned to speak to someone out in the hallway, then entered alone.

Fillet strutted to Kevin's desk, stopped abruptly. He looked at the ceiling. Kevin had never seen him so ill at ease.

"It's been a rough month, Michaels," he said, letting his ferret eyes meet Kevin's briefly, before breaking contact.

"Yes," Kevin answered. He pointed to the padded armchair inches from where Fillet stood. "Would you like to sit down?"

"No," Fillet said. "As I said, a very difficult month. We've lost Sidney Weiss to Northwestern, which was a blow, of course; and then there was the unpleasantness with your brief resignation . . ."

Kevin sensed a slight lifting of Fillet's spirits.

"And then, of course," Fillet went on, "we lost dear Henry Beardman to that madness last week. As well as yesterday, that student from your class . . ."

"Nicholas Backman."

"Yes, young Backman. Horrible."

Horrible, Kevin thought, *because Backman's father, who had bought his son's admission, will no longer be providing money to the university.*

Kevin waited patiently as Fillet's uneasiness returned.

"It's . . . not that I want to do this," Fillet said finally. His eyes returned from their wandering, zeroed in on Kevin's. "But it seems that John Groteman's decision on your reinstatement was premature. There was an inquiry . . ." Fillet could not keep the smirk off his face. "It seems there was a prior case that takes precedence, something in the Economics Department in 1957. I'm afraid your resignation will have to stand."

"Raymond—" Kevin began.

Fillet's hand went up. "This time it's irreversible, Michaels. Things must end somewhere. President Groteman has ruled."

Fillet waved Charles Steadman into the room from the hallway. Steadman wore a superior grin along with his tailored clothes and T. S. Eliot affectations. "Young Steadman here was, I thought, very unjustly treated to begin with. He will, as of this afternoon, take your place permanently on the faculty. It's only right, Michaels; and, I believe . . ."

Again Fillet's uneasiness returned, intensifying as Kevin rose and walked around his desk to face him.

"I . . . think you will agree," Fillet blustered, "that the only way to handle these things is through proper channels.

The department head should have his say, and well, that's what I've had in this matter—"

Kevin raised his hand as if to strike him. Fillet flinched, and, Kevin was pleased to note, Steadman stepped back, eyes wide, his own hands mute at his side.

Kevin turned, began to gather the papers on his desk. "I'll be out in an hour," he said.

"Fine," Fillet said quickly. "You're a fair man, Michaels. I expect no trouble. If, in the near future, an opening should occur—in fact, if, perhaps, the man I have in mind to fill Henry Beardman's spot is unavailable, we would of course be happy to have you back here, at least on a temporary basis, while we looked—"

"Please leave," Kevin said.

"Surely," Fillet stammered. "You have things to do. It's been a pleasure . . ."

Kevin listened to no more. Fillet's words faded until the door had been closed.

Twenty minutes later, Kevin was packing when the phone rang.

"Yes?"

"Kevin Michaels?"

"Yes." He noticed the agitation in the female voice.

"Mr. Michaels, this is New Polk County Hospital. Eileen Connel is a patient here. Someone . . . assaulted Ms. Connel in her room. It's horrible, but apparently her daughter has been murdered. Ms. Connel is insisting on seeing you, Mr. Michaels, and, well . . ."

"I'll be there in ten minutes," Kevin said.

"Thank you, Mr. Michaels. I'm afraid . . ." The voice paused. "I'm afraid Ms. Connel is dying."

•   •   •

She was surrounded by tubes and machines. At first, he didn't see her; the bed looked freshly made, flat, unoccupied. But she was in it, covers tucked at her chin, her thin face swollen with bruises, her thin white hair pushed carelessly back from her forehead.

"Eileen," he said.

He thought she was dead. A machine registered her heartbeat, but her skin was gray, lifeless.

She opened her eyes.

"Eileen," he said again.

She whispered something. As he bent closer, he realized that it was his name.

"Yes," he said.

She held up her hand, paper thin. There were bruises, bandages, up and down her arm.

She took his hand, tried to squeeze. Weakly, she pulled him down toward her.

"Listen," she whispered faintly.

She paused, closed her eyes, breathed deeply. She appeared to be battling herself.

"Eileen—" Kevin began.

Her eyes opened, focused on him. "I . . . It's going to be very difficult for me to keep my mind clear."

She drew in a long breath, closed her eyes. Her mouth twitched. She spoke something that sounded like a command to herself, *"Stay here."* Kevin moved closer, standing over her chair.

She opened her startling gray eyes. "I remember, Kevin."

He watched her eyes drift. She held his hand tighter, tried to rise. "No . . . Don't you *dare* raise your hand to me, Danny Sullivan! Go live in New York City! Get out!"

A tremor ran through her. She settled back, clenching her teeth. She hissed, said, "Stay . . ."

When she opened her eyes again, they were clear.

"That boy in jail," she whispered, "he didn't kill those

people. James Weston killed them. Lydia, too. Ask the boy where to find James Weston."

"Eileen," Kevin said. "You—"

"Listen to me!" Again she closed her eyes, clenched her teeth in effort.

She opened her eyes, reached her hand up to claw at Kevin's shoulder. "I told you, I remember! The thing in James Weston is the same thing that was in Jerry Martin. It was in me! That was how I learned."

"Eileen, I can't—"

Her grip tightened. "Listen to me! That was *Season of Witches*. That was where it came from. A thief . . ." Her eyes were hard and clear. "That was how I learned, Kevin."

"What did you learn?" he said quietly.

"Find James Weston. You have to destroy the thing inside him. It's . . ." She stiffened, fought to control herself.

Kevin gripped Eileen Connel by the shoulder, held her. "Tell me what you learned, Eileen."

Her eyes were hard as ice. "Promise me you'll find James Weston."

Kevin gripped her tight. "I will. Tell me."

Her gaze softened.

Kevin saw the erratic beat of her heart on the monitor. Ashamed, he bent his ear down to her, eagerly.

"You already have it," she whispered. "Jerry Martin just . . . made me see it."

"Eileen, what—?"

She smiled up at him, closed her eyes. The monitor showed a straight line, began to sound its alarm that she was dead.

"I love you, Kevin. . . ."

"I hear they're moving you tomorrow."

From the bed at the back of his cell, knees pulled up,

Davey Putnam regarded Kevin Michaels with a sullenness that closely resembled dulled fear. There were bruises on his face. His seeming uncaring attitude was undercut by a wariness detectable in his sharp eyes.

"I said, they're moving you tomorrow," Kevin repeated. The boy said nothing.

"Don't you care?"

"How did you get in here?" the boy asked.

"I told the cop out front I was from your attorney's office."

"You lied."

"Yes."

Kevin detected a heightening of the boy's interest. "Why?"

"Maybe you didn't do what they say you did."

"Are you a reporter?"

"No. But will you be very frank with me?" Kevin asked.

"Maybe."

"Maybe isn't good enough."

Davey rose from the bed. Kevin saw that one eye was blackened, nearly closed. The boy came to the bars of the cell, gripped them hard, pressed his face between them. "James Weston is going to kill me."

"They say you killed him, and hid his body somewhere."

"He killed them all!" The boy's fear was so palpable Kevin felt the hairs on the back of his neck rise.

The door at the far end of the long gray corridor opened. Officer Johnston put his head in, looked grimly at Kevin. "Everything all right?"

"Yes," Kevin said.

"Three more minutes and you're out."

"Fine."

Johnston glared at him, closed the door.

"Look," Kevin said to Davey. "They found your fingerprints all over Ben Meyer's house, on the shovel that buried the bodies, all over the Backman house, even on the knife in your friend's back and on the bag of cocaine in the cellar. That was all in the papers. The only way I could prove any of what you say is to find James Weston."

The boy looked at him steadily. "I don't know if I can trust you."

"Do you have a choice?"

The boy looked so suddenly young and helpless, so absent of bravado, that Kevin wanted to reach through the bars and hold him.

"The dog could find him," Davey said.

"What dog?"

"There was a dog with me. He knows James Weston."

"What happened to him?"

"He ran away when the police got to Nick Backman's house."

"Where would he be now?"

The door at the end of the corridor opened again. "That's it," Johnston's hard voice said.

Kevin looked at Davey. "Tell me where to look for the dog."

Davey hesitated. "All right," he said.

Davey dreamed he heard, through the gray, flat walls, the howl of the dog running. He imagined the dog tearing through the fields, something cold at his heels. But the dog was uncatchable.

Suddenly, the dog turned in midrun, twisted up into the air. His rusty-brown coat turned just behind his body, hair billowing. He caught the cold, stalking thing in his mouth, gripped its neck deep in his teeth, and closed. The stalking thing cried a hollow cry and fell back, throwing its deadened hands ineffectively to the sky—

He awoke.

Up on his elbows, the cold, hard wafer of mattress un-yielding. Tiny gray and white pinstripes, a hard starched sheet, an unfeathered pillow filled with broken foam. Light in the corridor.

"Time for your beating, Putnam."

Davey rose up to a sit, looked through the bars. The door at the corridor end opened, letting a tall, thin spill of light into the area.

Officer Johnston entered the corridor, billy club in hand. He shook the key ring on his belt. "I'm losing you tomor-row, so I'll have to make this one good."

Another figure, taller, filled the doorway behind John-ston.

Johnston turned as the tall man's arm rose. Davey saw something bright, backlit, move in a flashing arc. Johnston's hands went to his throat . . .

The tall man pushed Johnston down, moved the knife through his neck. Johnston fell, made a gasp, was silent. The tall man let the knife fall with him.

Davey saw the tall man bend over the cop, remove the key ring from his belt.

The tall man straightened.

"No!" Davey shouted.

James Weston came toward his cell. Shadow-light showed the twin lines of suspenders over the shoulders.

"Someone help me!"

Weston's hands lay on the bars, like flat, dead, calm white slabs of meat. The head was half shadowed. There was the sound of shallow, deep breathing.

"Stay away," Davey said, retreating to the back of the cell.

Weston lifted the hand holding the key ring from the bars, bent to the lock, tried one key and then another. The third made a snapping metal sound as the lock disengaged.

"Jesus—help me!"

Weston pulled the cell door back on its hinges.

Kevin bolted forward, ducking under the arch of Weston's arm. A heavy hand landed on his back, knocked him to the floor.

"Jesus!"

Weston held him down, dragged him back into the cell. Davey writhed, trying to beat the tall man's arms off. Weston pushed him back, climbed on top of him, pinned him.

Davey whipped his head from side to side. "No!"

The tall man put the flats of his hands to Davey's head and squeezed, holding him.

"No!"

Davey closed his eyes, smelling Weston's putrid breath. *"No!"*

Davey opened his eyes wide. Weston's face was inches from his own. The eyes were flat, like painted plastic. The white, unsmiling flesh looked unliving.

"Help me!"

Weston covered Davey's mouth with his own. Davey couldn't move his head or breathe. He screamed into the hollow, damp cave of Weston's mouth.

Weston's tongue bridged his own. Something crawled into his mouth, dropped to the back of his throat, bored in—

At the instant of transference, Davey looked into Weston's eyes and saw the flat lifelessness replaced by bright light. As the face crumbled away, life burst back into the eyes.

Davey heard a shout of exhultation . . .

Davey screamed. Something said, *Fine.* Then the scream was pushed into the back of his throat, up into his head, and in despair, he felt himself stolen.

17
October 31st

Twilight, Halloween.

It should have been beautiful. Leaf colors, as if on cue, had reached peak: a blinding cascade of orange, yellow, red; and the trees, as if knowing it was the last day of October, that winter was close by, shook their branches in the blustering wind, letting loose a rain of color on the town.

Kevin's car window was down. The air was apple-chilled; the dropping night was blue-black and clear. The smell of burning leaves smoldering in a caged trash can coupled with the cold smell of stars.

It should have been beautiful. Trick-or-treaters swarmed in packs, waved bags, kicked through leaves: witches, ghosts, spacemen, monsters. Houses were guarded by pumpkins, flickering triangle eyes, sickle-grin mouths with the waning heat of candle stumps. Pumpkin tops smoldered black, smelled like burned pumpkin pies.

Pumpkin cutouts filled windows. Jointed skeletons hung from doors. On one house, white clapboard, deep-green shutters, a zombie cutout was taped to the picture window, stiff arms outstretched, face powdered, eyes wide, empty as black wells—

A stray cat, appropriately black, froze in Kevin's headlights. He braked. The cat hissed, arched its back, glared at him with green eyes. It dashed over the curb, rattled between two trash cans . . .

It should have been beautiful.

But it wasn't. The portentous boom of the last movement of Brahms's Fourth Symphony filled the car's cassette deck.

A push of cold wind splashed leaves on the road in front of Kevin.

He shivered.

He stopped for a light, heard a call of laughter. He watched a group of costumed children cross the street in front of him, bags rustling, capes moving. They entered a bar called the Swan, pushed like wraiths through the front door under the awning. He heard them call "Trick or treat!" as the tavern door swung shut behind them. A moment later they were herded out, laughing, a slim man holding a towel, scowling, telling them, "Go on. Play your tricks somewhere else."

The light changed. The town thinned away behind Kevin. There were empty, rutted rows of stems, rotting pumpkins, a closed farmstand cloaked in shadow.

He pulled to the curb, turned off the engine.

Brahms, on a full, high note of doom, went silent.

He got out of the car, headed into the field.

Dry dirt puffed up. Dry stalks, green, dead, twisted pumpkin vines, cut clean at the ends or ripped away, reached at him, tried to trip him. A huge, fat, ripe pumpkin faced him; as he passed it, the back was visible, kicked in, a spill of pulp, clustered white seeds, ruin . . .

The farmstand was behind him. He found the path into the hill.

He climbed.

At the top of the hill he stopped, spellbound. It should have been beautiful. New Polk lay out for him on a plate below. Leaves fell on perfectly paved streets. Stately oaks arched protectively. He saw the university, red brick and clocktower, a white, round face with black stick arms at six o'clock. He heard the distant bell. The leafy emptiness of the quadrangle, just glimpsed. Houses spread around the college like ranked gems, tar-shingle roofs, white clapboard, shutters like brows on their windows, reflecting orange night.

Tears came into his eyes.

It should have been beautiful.

He stumbled on, cutting left toward the orchard, keeping the ridgeline until he entered the trees.

Here, in the nightshade of these bare branches, autumn had already passed to winter. Dead apples. The ground was carpeted in unharvested fruit, saturated with the sharp, sick smell of rot. Insects moved into fruit corpses, drilled holes into paling red skins. Pulp turned from crisp white to soft mealiness. Brown, the color of decay.

He moved through apples, stepped on apples, could not avoid apples.

He stopped, listened.

The silence of failing autumn. Wind clicked the branches. Dry limbs, like a cornfield. He turned his collar up. There was a dotting of bright stars overhead.

Twilight gave in to night.

Through the crooked, framing arms of trees, he watched New Polk blink its night eyes open. Halloween porches. Candles snugged and lit into sweet floors of pumpkins.

Dripping wax. A blow of scent through the eyeholes, dancing flames . . .

He listened for the dog.

Colder, windy. His collar was not enough. He shivered. Fear rose into him. The unseen: a tall man in suspenders, a stiff white shirt. In the trees? He glanced up. A thousand hiding places.

Again, he listened for the dog.

He stopped.

Ahead, a flitting presence in the dark. Watching him, wary. He could feel it.

A star, bright Vega, winked between two low, wind-whipped branches, cradled the horizon.

A crawling feeling up his back. He turned. In a clear lane between trees, the rising fatness of the moon, an orange presence, pumpkin in the sky, pulled itself above New Polk.

A taffy-pull of clouds moved across its surface.

Nearby, a dog sound, mournful, deep in the throat. Careful, mistrusting.

He looked toward the sound.

The dog moved out from behind the bole of a gray tree. It was hobbled. The right front paw was damaged, collapsing at each step. The dog's eyes were bright; it showed its teeth, barked a warning.

"I'm not going to hurt you," Kevin said. He knelt, held a hand out. "Davey told me to find you."

The dog hobbled forward, stopped ten feet away, still wary.

"Come on," Kevin said.

The dog sniffed, moved forward, sniffed again.

"That's it."

Abruptly the dog made the last four steps, laid its head in Kevin's outstretched hand, sat heavily, sighing.

"Good dog." Kevin ruffled the dog's deep coat behind the ears. "Good boy."

The dog lifted its head, peered into the darkness, let its head fall again. It sighed, a huffing sound.

"I need you."

The dog made a deep, content sound. Kevin thought the dog had gone to sleep. He turned over the dog's right front paw, found a raw, skinned spot just above the pad, extending up the bone.

The dog tried to rise.

"Hold on," Kevin said.

He made the dog sit, pulled out his shirttail from under his jacket, worked at it, tore a strip of cloth. "Let's see what we can do."

The dog settled, closed its eyes, let Kevin work.

Easy.

That's what it would be. Already he enjoyed the new body, the young boy's relative strength, the endurance of pain, the fast legs. The boy's youth only added to his prowess, would make it easier to leap, to grasp, to choke, to kill. Perfect for tonight. And the boy would be blamed for everything.

In sheer exhilaration, he retrieved the key ring next to the dusty clothes, the red-stained shirt, the suspenders, that had been James Weston's. He ran through the police station, unlocked the rifle case, removed a twelve-gauge shotgun, plenty of shells.

Then—out into the night.

My night!

He made the boy's face smile widely, excitedly, because that was the way he felt. The moon rising up. Everything meshed like a perfect machine.

It was almost like it had been.

My night!

He would make it as close as he could. A singing rushed

through him, through the body. He jumped into the air, shouted, "Yes!" It felt good.

A man approached. Medium height, balding, impatient walk. Alone. The man looked at him strangely. Darkness between buildings. The man saw the shotgun, stopped, tried to put a look of blankness on his face, which didn't mask his sudden fear.

He made the young boy's body jump again. "Yes!" In midjump he realized the boy knew this man. *Who?* Foster father.

The boy hated him—ole Jack.

Fine.

"Yes!" He completed the jump. As he touched ground directly in front of the man, he snugged the shotgun under the man's chin and pulled both triggers.

Yes!

The man flew back, a shower of blood, twitching to the ground.

He ran on, reloaded the shotgun.

My night!

The corner of a building. A woman appeared, walked across his path, bundled against the chill. A grocery bag, plastic bag of candy topping it.

"Yes!"

He aimed for her face near the bag top, pulled one trigger, watched her hands fly out, drop the groceries.

But he had only grazed the front of her face. The open bag of candy spilled on the pavement. He pointed the barrel down, carefully this time, pulled off the other shell.

"Perfect!"

A perfect night.

My night.

This was what he missed. When he had been content to be served, it had been like this. *A god,* they had called him. What better station than to be a god? To be held in godhood by an inferior race. The plague, human beings overrunning the earth. The dinosaurs. He should have stopped the human race, too.

An old rage was filling him, drowning his exhilaration. Why did his own die? Godhood had been his consolation.

He remembered that first time, the lonely boring up through the endless mother earth to the surface. The first contact, the first taking over. They were like babies to him, their pliant minds, accessible wills. Easy to own.

Soon, they had feared, worshiped him.

The birds, the fishes, he had been their god, too.

And then, the humans had left him behind.

What was left but rage?

He found himself screaming. He filled the boy's mouth with raw hate. He stopped before a door. It opened almost immediately at his knock. A frightened face. A teenage girl; he saw the candy bowl on a nearby table. A staircase behind it led up. Hallway straight ahead, glimpse of a kitchen. The door closed, the wood pushed against him.

"Open this now!" he shrieked. He kicked, the door burst back, meeting a chain. He jammed two shells into the shotgun, rammed the door.

He heard a heavier voice, foot treads, coming toward him.

He aimed at the chain, blew it off the door, kicked the door open. He faced a large man, shirtsleeves, receding hairline, glasses, dress pants, newspaper clutched in one hand.

The man raised a finger to point as he fired the second barrel into the face. He cocked the shotgun open, fed shells to it. More shouts through the house. A loud television. A commercial ended, music out of a haunted house.

He marched down the hallway.

The teenage girl in the kitchen was sunk to her knees, phone receiver to her ear. He fired off one shot. More commotion; the stairs in the front, someone banging down them.

A woman's scream; a weaker one. The mother turned to see him advance from the kitchen. She clutched a child to her, in costume, round plastic bear mask, smiling. One shot at the mother.

The boy let her go, ran for the front door, arms out-stretched.

"Yes!"

Some of his enthusiasm returned. One careful shot in the back. The boy went down, mask twisted off by the impact.

He stepped over the bodies, reloaded, moved on.

The dog could walk. Kevin didn't know what they would do if they had to run. But the dog was less hobbled now.

The dog voiced its thanks by laying its head in Kevin's hand. It made a sound nearly like a purr.

"Good boy," Kevin said.

Kevin followed the dog out of the back of the orchard to a rock wall. The dog held back. Kevin climbed, lifted the dog over.

"Okay."

The dog huffed, went ahead of him, led down an un-perceived trail. Kevin stumbled after in moonlight, holding his collar against the wind.

The bus station loomed into view. A bus was just pulling out, windows dark as slate. Pity. They would escape. When did the next bus leave? A half hour?

Never.

He smiled.

Perhaps, one day, he would tire of his game, his piece-meal destruction of a foolish race, and do them all in at once. Occasionally, he thought of it. A chain of command, a line of used bodies until he obtained one with a finger who could push the button. Even in their moment of holocaust, they would blame one another. After watching the beginning, the first tall radioactive clouds tearing up into the atmosphere, as the eyes of his inhabited body were burned out, he would drop out of the screaming mouth, burrow deep into mother earth, and await renewal. How long would it take? Years? Centuries? What would he find when he surfaced? A new race of mutations, swarming like insects over a ruined landscape? Nothing at all? What would he live on? Wouldn't that be the loneliest existence of all?

Could he live in a world alone, without even these sluglike humans?

The boy's body shivered.

Wasn't it better to live like this, killing them slowly, using them, making them pay for all eternity for their abdication of his godhood?

"Yes!" he said, holding the shotgun up like a trophy.

He walked into the gas station next to the bus depot, crossed the median until he came to the nearest pump. He removed the pump head from its socket, flipped the switch, then locked the handle in an open position and began to pump gas out onto the tarmac.

Someone shouted. A young man was running from the filling-station office, greased fatigues, cap pushed back on his head. The attendant had a soda in one hand.

Davey laid the pumping nozzle carefully on the ground, turned, aimed the shotgun, fired one barrel.

The attendant clawed at his chest, collapsed.

Davey turned. A woman stared at him, her own gassing complete, pocketbook open.

He fired the other barrel.

He opened and reloaded the shotgun, walked to where the woman lay on the tarmac. He found her car keys in her bag and pocketed them. Another car was just entering the island; the driver looked out at the woman on the ground.

Davey aimed one barrel through the driver's window. The driver screamed, threw his hands to his face. The car swerved, banged one of the gas pumps hard enough to dislodge it from its base. A line of gas ran from the bottom, pooled, grew.

Davey walked from pump to pump, turned them on, locked them. The island was awash in petrol.

Davey went to the woman's car, got in, started it. Vehicles were stopping in the street, drivers straining to see.

Davey pulled out to the street, stopped, rolled down his window. He pointed the shotgun back at the pool of gas, pulled the trigger.

A rushing ball of fire shot up into the air, rolled around on itself, then fell to consume the gas station. Cars honked their horns, stopped in the middle of the road.

The garage in the gas station caught fire. A tongue of flame shot next door to the bus depot. The pool of gas, still alive, ran into the street, beneath a bus. The bus's gas tank exploded, lifting the vehicle up off its rear wheels.

Davey pulled away, drove until he found a darkened corner with another gas station on it. In a kiosk, a lone attendant sat reading a paper, pooled in neon light, leaning back in his chair.

Davey pulled in, braked, got out of the car. He unhooked all the pump heads from their moorings, locked them into position, turned the levers on. Nothing happened. His eyes traveled across the gas pump, read, PLEASE PAY BEFORE PUMPING.

He approached the kiosk, shot the attendant as he was rising, leaned over the body, switched on the pump register.

Outside, gas spurted from all the open nozzles.

Davey ran back to the car, dodging gasoline flows, got in, shot at the petrol, drove away.

A roar of fire went up behind him.

He lit three more stations in quick succession, nearly ringing the town.

By the time he heard he first fire engine siren, the wind was already helping.

Kevin was halfway down the hill leading into town when he heard a *whump.*

The sky brightened on the far side of New Polk. There was a second explosion, more decisive. A dart of pumpkin-colored flame rose, fell back.

A dim orange glow capped an area near the university. It didn't diminish. Soon, it grew.

"Jesus," Kevin said.

Another *whump* sounded, east of the first. A ball of fire was thrown into the air, settled back, drew toward the first. Firelight began to overtake moonlight.

Kevin started to run down the hillside.

In the distance, he heard screams.

Another *whump.* A half-circle of fire wrapped the out-skirts of New Polk, moved inward with the wind. Kevin felt a shimmer of distant heat on his face. Another explosion sounded, nearly completing the fire circle of the town.

"My God," Kevin said, watching in awe as the conflagra-tion, fed by wind and oxygen, built to a firestorm.

A lone siren went off, stopped in midwail.

Not many would escape. No one in this foolish town could possibly know the workings of a firestorm, the terrible, quick, inescapable trap.

He had seen enough firestorms, of course; in Germany, in Japan. Once, in Tokyo, in the days just before the atomic bomb, he had watched, inhabiting the body of a young Japa-nese girl, as Curtis LeMay's planes completely missed their targets. Most of their incendiary bombs fell harmlessly into the water. But he had, with the help of the girl's body, placed a few well-set fires into the wind, then watched those paperlike houses go up, feed on one another. Before it was over, a half-mile section of the city had burned to ashes.

Those were not good days, the war. They killed so many of themselves he had felt deprived. So, for a time, he had played one of his other games, riding a single human for years at a time to dissolution. Sometimes he used drugs, sometimes alcohol, or sex. For a while he enjoyed watching the depths to which a human being could be driven: bestiality, necrophilia. As with that Japanese girl . . .

Of course, he had, riding humans, traveled everywhere, done it all before: in ancient Greece, in Rome; and in early Britain, when the Celts had made him a god, and later, when they had transmogrified and merely feared him. He thought of the devil worshipers he had ridden, been among; only the mad ones paid homage to him, now. . . .

He smelled burning leaves, burning oak wood, and a fresh rage filled him. The Celts had burned oak for him. He hadn't realized how much he missed true godhood.

Perhaps he could have it again.

He had one final task before he could climb the hills outside New Polk and enjoy his Druidic bonfire. Driving fast, avoiding cars filled with panicking drivers, he screeched to a halt in front of the huge, open garage doors of the firehouse. Its siren, mounted on a high pole outside, screamed.

He got out of the car, walked to the open doorway, looked in. Men in black slickers were loading their trucks frantically with equipment. The hook-and-ladder driver was already mounted. He leaned from the window of his cab, yelled impatiently for his fellows to finish their work.

Two firemen hopped onto the rear of the truck, signaled

their readiness. The driver in the cab put the diesel into roaring life, threw the truck into gear.

He saw Davey blocking the truck, braked, leaned out of the window.

"Get the hell out of the way! Are you crazy!" he yelled.

Davey walked to the fire truck, hoisted himself up on the running board.

The fireman put his arm out, pointing. "Move that goddamn car—"

Davey shoved the shotgun into his neck and fired.

Two firemen jumped down from the back of the truck, walked forward. Davey stepped off the running board, shot one of them. The man went down, holding his thigh. The other ran.

Davey calmly reloaded. He walked to the back of the fire truck, found the large, silver-colored gas-tank cover, twisted it open. It fell off, hanging on its chain. He tore strips of cloth from his shirt, tied them end to end. He led one end deep into the fuel tank and pulled it out, soaked. He led in the other end of the strip.

"Don't, man!"

The fireman he had shot in the thigh stared at him from the floor. Davey raised the shotgun, fired. The man was silent. Davey walked to the body, searched the pockets, came up with a book of matches.

Appropriate.

He went to the other fire truck, uncovered the gas tank, soaked another length of cloth. He lit a match, touched it to the soaked rag, walked to the hook and ladder, repeated the operation.

He went back to the street, got into the car, pulled out. A half block away, as he headed for the hole in the bottleneck that had become hell in New Polk, he heard the firehouse siren go mute.

There was a booming explosion in the center of New Polk. Standing on the road in front of the farmstand, Kevin was blinded. Waves of heat flowed out at him. A wall of fire rode the wind like a hinge, was slamming the town shut.

A single car tore out of the closing flames, its rear edged in fire. It skidded on the road, hit the far curb as the gas tank exploded. The automobile was engulfed in flames.

Kevin ran toward the car. A second explosion sounded, under the front hood. The engine blew free, landed twisting on the roadway. Screams within were silenced.

Kevin approached, saw a feeble arm in the front seat stop moving, covered in fire, turn black. A face fell toward the open window, dead, burning—Raymond Fillet.

"Jesus."

The rear windows blew out, pushing fire out at Kevin, the scent of roasting flesh. There was a final scream, and Kevin saw the visage of Charles Steadman push out of the window, seeking oxygen, before collapsing dead into the blazing interior.

A sound. Kevin turned. Another car roared through the flames, untouched. Behind it, the door shut, walls of fire climbing up one another in greeting, fusing into a solid barricade.

The car thundered past, braked thirty yards beyond in a slicing skid. It reversed, slowly backed toward Kevin.

The dog's ears went back. It tensed on its haunches, growled angrily.

The car stopped ten yards away, the door opened.

Davey Putnam got out.

"Davey!" Kevin cried.

The dog barked savagely.

Kevin said to the dog, "It's Davey!"

"Yes, it's me, Rusty," Davey said.

The dog ran forward, leaped as Davey drew his shotgun from behind his back.

As the dog struck, Davey fired.

The shot took Rusty in the hind legs. His angry growl turned to a wail of pain.

Howling with rage and hurt, the dog tore at Davey Putnam's neck. Davey beat at the dog with his fists, tried to pull it off by the back of the head. He tried to angle the shotgun up but could not. He dropped the gun and put both hands on the dog's head, tried to twist it away from his neck.

The dog held on as Kevin approached. Blood poured from the dog's leg wounds, running down Davey Putnam's front. Davey tore at the dog's face, pulled its mouth apart, angled his thumbs at the dog's eyes. Still the dog persisted.

A wheezing sound began in the back of Davey Putnam's throat. His hands tightened convulsively on the dog's head, ripped it away from his throat.

The dog fell to the ground, panting, paws limp.

Davey Putnam's eyes glazed. Blood roared from his neck. His hands dropped to his sides. He lay back against the side of the car, wheezing through his torn windpipe.

The dog was silent, eyes ruined.

Kevin went to it and bent down.

The dog looked blindly at Kevin, huffed wanly, tried to lift its head.

"Take it easy, boy," Kevin said. He put his hand on the dog's head, moved it to scratch him affectionately behind the ears.

"Y—" Davey Putnam said.

Kevin turned as Davey Putnam's hand fell hard on him, taking him in an unbreakable grip, pulling him down.

"Y—You," Davey Putnam's ruined mouth whispered. "Y—"

"Let me go!"

Davey's grip hardened. He pulled Kevin down toward him, forced him over onto his back. Davey moved on top of Kevin's struggling body, held him down, pressed his hands into Kevin's neck. He moved them to the sides of Kevin's head and squeezed.

Kevin watched Davey's face, frozen, dead looking, eyes flat as stone, lower toward his own. A weak, mewling sound came from behind the tightly closed lips.

Suddenly, for the merest instant, Davey's eyes cleared, filled in with life. "Don't . . . let him!" Davey's real, ragged voice shouted.

The light left the eyes. Slowly, Davey's face moved up over him, turned to the side. Kevin watched the open, bleeding neck wound lower toward his mouth.

"No!" Kevin screamed.

Something small moved in the ruined, pulpy, bloody flesh of Davey's neck, pulled itself out of the wound.

Davey Putnam's thumbs forced Kevin's mouth open.

Davey Putnam's neck lowered to Kevin's mouth. Kevin felt the claw of something on his lip, over his tongue, moving back, a pinch up at the back of his throat—

Kevin felt himself pushed inward, compacted away from his extremities, taken away from himself . . .

Yes! He found new purchase; instantly, he saw that all would be well. A good body, young, more than acceptable. His ride out of New Polk. On to . . . Michigan?

Yes! He saw already what he would do. Kevin Michaels would leave New Polk unscathed. Lucky survivor! And . . . he had been on his way to leaving, anyway. Excellent! A new home in academia, Northwestern University, a teaching position, perhaps. Sidney Weiss would help him. A scholar! Devotee of Eileen Connel!

The same Kevin Michaels who spurned Eileen Connel's daughter, Lydia!

How . . . apt!

He was becoming comfortable already. He would ride this one for a while. He had rather enjoyed his last travel, across the country on foot. Perhaps he would make Kevin Michaels walk also, see the United States before settling down in Michigan. There would be no boredom along the way—a traveling academic could get away with plenty without detection. Kevin Michaels was clean-cut, respectable, hardly a suspect.

But how to handle his role as only survivor of the New Polk conflagration? Ah. Perhaps an exhausted rest in the field next to the farmstand. The scenario: The neighboring towns, who would soon respond, would find the sole survivor weeping tears of loss, wailing over the horror he has witnessed, his town burned to ashes, the bones of his friends mixed with the earth, turned to fertilizer, gone. An excellent mind, this Kevin Michaels! He would enjoy this; perhaps he would return to a quieter existence, ride this body to ruin, draw pleasure from the slow extinction of Kevin Michaels.

Yes! And here a perfect place to rest. Off the highway, in the shadow of the lonely farmstand, a furrow of picked pumpkins.

Lay thee down, Kevin Michaels, to rest amidst the severed stems of your dreams—

Kevin felt something like a dentist's drill go through him, finding a hidden nerve in his sleep, waking him up. He was yanked instantly from foggy nothingness, looked out momentarily through his own eyes again. The smell of burning leaves, burning oak. New Polk, burning.

He felt pain. How did he get hurt? In his battle with Davey Putnam? Where was Davey Putnam?

He looked down, saw empty folds of clothing, a spill of white dust.

It's inside me.

The thing in his limbs, crowning his mind like a spider, said to him, *Yes. I just want to look you over.*

He cried out, but it didn't reach his lips. He felt himself being pushed back to numbness again, receding from his own hands and legs. From his own mind. The pain was receding, too.

"No!"

He held on to the pain, magnified it, bathed in it. He pushed the pain into every corner of his body until he heard himself scream.

He willed his hand to move, searched along the back of his own leg, found the source of the pain. The mouth of the dog was clamped to him.

He looked down at the dog. It was barely breathing, eyes glazed, holding desperately on.

"Good . . ." Kevin said.

He dug his finger past the dog's straining teeth, down into his own open wound.

He screamed aloud, felt himself flood back to the edges of his being.

Me.

He sat up, felt the thing in his mouth clawing desperately within, trying to keep hold. The dog lay dead beside him in the furrow, blinded eyes turned upward.

Good dog.

The thing in his mouth scrambled, held his tongue in its pincers, pulled itself back toward the back of his throat—

What is this!

The dog again. He saw it from the corner of Kevin Michaels's eye as Michaels wrenched control from him. The jolt of anguish through him, he had been foolish, had not gained control, had stopped to revel in victory, instead of boring all the way in. Fool! Now he lost contact, was thrown into the front of Kevin Michaels's mouth.

Quickly! He turned himself, dug in, pulled himself back. But now he was being fought, and he screamed—

Kevin opened his mouth. The thing in his throat lost grip, hit the roof of his mouth, scraped along it to hit his teeth. Tiny pincers tapped them like metal.

Kevin pushed out with his tongue, felt the thing fighting to take hold. The thing dropped to his tongue, scrabbled back—

Kevin's mind clouded, cleared, clouded again. He felt himself torn between two worlds. He felt the thing snaring him, digging into his head, trying to compact him. He looked down, saw the hard furrows, his own shoes, the world pulling down away as if he had been shot up in a rocket—

His mind clouded.

"Rrrrrrrraaaaa," he heard his mouth say from a distance. *"Rrrrraaaaaaaa."*

He could not even speak his own screams.

Me!

He whirled, willed his legs to work. Far off, the back of his leg ached. He willed his hand down to the spot, dug his fingers like claws into the wound.

He screamed, became himself again. He saw he was at the back of Packer's Farmstand.

Now, he thought.

"Rrrrraaaa, rrrraaaa."

He opened his mouth wide, forced his shaking fingers up, moved them in and back. He began to gag. His fingers brushed something hard, moving. For a moment he went blind, then suddenly his mind cleared completely. He was flooded with pain and sensibility, making him scream his own screams of joy—

This is what she meant!

Me!

No more!

An alarm went off, telling him to give up. This had happened before. There was not enough contact in Kevin Michaels's head. There was too much chance of danger. His sense of self-preservation set in.

He dropped from the back of Kevin Michaels's throat, slid out over the tongue and through the screaming mouth, fell to the ground, began to dig.

Another day . . .

A shame it could not ride Kevin Michaels, watch him suffer.

Another day . . .

He would return. Kevin Michaels would know his revenge, as Eileen Connel had. It was time to move on, now. But, someday, he would ride back . . .

Through a haze of joy, Kevin Michaels saw the thing tumble to the ground, begin to bore voraciously into the earth.

ME!

Kevin fell to his knees, overwhelmed. He felt himself burst like fire to the very limits of himself. His fingertips, his eyes, his tongue, the dermal layers of his skin, burned with life.

Me!

He gasped. He felt more alive than he ever imagined he could, as if he had been thrown at this instant, fully sensate, into the world. He trembled with aliveness; a tingle spread out through him, electric, life itself.

ME!

His eye caught movement in the dirt below him. The thing, the evil thing, was boring down into the earth.

Kevin dug his fingers (My fingers! Feel them! Feel their wonderful life!) into the hole after it.

It squirmed down, away from him.

Get it.

He stood, unsteady on his legs, still gasping, and looked around himself. At the back of the farmstand was a rack of tools, a shovel. He stumbled to it, knocking into a cartful of apples, artfully arranged.

Apples (smell them! Their beautiful odor! The world, the whole world, alive!) spilled to the ground.

Dig! Kevin Michaels told himself.

Bearing the shovel, feeling the smooth wood through his fingers (my fingers! Feel them!), he staggered back to the thing's hole, angled the shovel into it, pushed in the blade—

Hurry! Now he must dig deep into the earth, the mother, where he would rest. A fearful rage went through him. How dare Kevin Michaels! A hate, purer than any he had ever felt, coursed through him. He would make Kevin Michaels pay, would make all these humans pay. Suddenly he had decided: All of them must die. The humans were too much a plague. He would brush them clean from the earth. He could risk them no more. Everything they had ascribed to him, godhood, satanic majesty, awe, fear—all of it was gone. That could not happen! And when he did away with them all, he would make sure the human race knew Kevin Michaels was the cause. A phone call from the president, the button pushed, twisting the man's insides, making him weep, say, "It was *you,* Kevin, it was *you . . ."*

The earth would abide. He would abide. He could even see himself playing with any survivors, torturing the mutations he had created, a whole new race of his own making.

Yes!

He dug, hungrily.

Dig.

The only thing that mattered was digging. Kevin's arms ached beautifully—deep throbs down in the muscles below his chilled flesh. He felt each sensation, each movement, each pump of blood. The back of his leg was painfully afire. He relished it.

Dig.

The hole deepened. He spaded another rush of black loam onto his shovel and lifted it high above his head, dropping it out of the hole. The smell of pungent earth mixed with burning leaves and oak wood snaked into his nostrils, a beautiful, full sensation—

Me!

Dig.

He angled the shovel, pushed it downward—

He stopped. In the loose dirt, something twisted, dug down away from him.

Quickly, ignoring the tightening pain in his forearms, he pierced soil with shovel blade, pressed down.

Outside, around him, the cold night brightened with orange light. His eyes, oversensitive, drank it in. The smell of burning leaves impregnated the taut, cold air, wafted away.

Something moved against the blade of the shovel, tapped, and squirmed away. He forced the blade down and felt it trapped, fighting for release.

Yes!

The sky in front of Kevin was on fire. He felt insistent movement against the shovel. He looked down to see the thing's head pulling away from the shovel blade, curling down into the loam, leaving a wake of churned, moist soil behind.

He brought the shovel up to his eyes, stared at the smooth U cut out of the steel blade at the tip.

Dig!

The smell of burning leaves reached achingly across his nostrils again. This was life, all of it was life, flooding into him. This was what Eileen knew, what Brahms sensed—even in death, life. A flood of life.

He jammed the shovel back into the dirt. His aching muscles were joy. Cold sweat beaded his face.

The shovel split earth, lifted dirt, drove down, split earth again.

He shivered in pain and cold and joy. The shovel blade drove, lifted, drove—caught.

Again, he felt movement against the blade.

The thing's head bored up from the dark loam. One of its tiny, jointed legs pushed up, waved like an antenna before moving against the shovel blade, scraping methodically at it up and down.

The thing stared up at his face.

It was slug colored, reptilian. Its long, thin tail ended in a tiny, split fork. Behind its head were the merest bumps, the hint of horns. Its small, round mouth opened and closed like a gasping, prehistoric fish. Its eyes were round, slightly raised, dark, blank, like gray wens.

He watched the thing work against the shovel. The muscles in Kevin's arms, his legs, his back, felt like stretches of molten lead.

He felt cold night-sweat on his skin, smelled the odor of burning leaves, mingled now with the odor of shingles and insulation and car metal, the burning flesh of men—

Even this is life. Death is life. I own even my own death, it belongs to me, makes part of my whole.

I AM ME.

Now, he told himself.

Eyes averted, one shivering hand keeping firm pressure on the shovel, he reached down and took hold of the thing. He released pressure on the shovel. The thing came gently free of the soil. Its many legs pulled up from the dirt, curling tightly around his fingers. He felt the thing's tail whip across his knuckles. His thumb brushed across the thing's face; he felt the tiny mouth opening and closing, trying to bite.

Do it, he told himself.

He held the thing before his face, not looking at it.

He opened his mouth and put it in.

Caught!

The thing went wild with fury. He was caught, was being lifted from the soil! *Fight!* He moved his tiny claws ineffectively against the human's finger.

Millenniums would not end like this! He would not let it happen!

What was this! Its tiny eyes saw the human's mouth opening, saw himself going in—

Find purchase! Catch hold!

Kevin Michaels held the thing in his mouth. It let go of his fingers, strained for his tongue, tried to scrape its legs into it.

Now.

I am life, he thought. *I am me.*

Kevin brought his teeth together.

WHAT IS HE DOING!

.   .   .

Kevin's mouth filled with burning liquid. *Acid.* A thousand, a million memories, not his own, washed over him, were gone. He felt Davey Putnam flow through him, released. The history of mankind, an evil, endless train back to the caves, the trees, a rushing line of hate and death. The memories flashed to brilliance; he saw a cold field, men with horned masks, a huge pyre of burning sticks, a human slave within, screaming for release. He saw the dark sky burn, the color of pumpkin . . .

ALL IS LOST! It felt its legs pull away from its mind, the fade of its existence, spiraling at last toward the end . . .

Its tiny eyes looked out; saw the pyre of orange flame rising in the night, saw the burning of the world, the sacrifice, just for itself . . .

I WAS A GOD!

Kevin collapsed, gasping. The pictures let him go. He was himself, all himself, and he lay touching his hand with his own hand. He touched his face.

He was not dead.

He felt wonderfully exhausted. He rolled over, looked at the burning-cloud sky, cold patches of night between. It was beautiful, all of it was beautiful.

Me.

Yes, Father.

Yes, Eileen.

He rose, stumbled to where Rusty lay dead. He collapsed beside the dog in the hard furrow of dead pumpkins. His eyes faced the burning town. He heard, far off but nearing, the wail of many sirens.

He turned his eyes away, closed them.

His body was suddenly very tired. He felt his hand fall on

the cold, furred body of the dog. In his head he heard sad, triumphant, human music that sounded like Brahms.

"Good dog," he whispered, closing his eyes.

This would be a good place for them to find him.

the cold body of the dog in his hand he heard that triumphant, human music that sounded like Brutus.

"Good boy," he whispered, closing his eyes.

About the Author

AL SARRANTONIO's forty short stories have appeared in such magazines as *Heavy Metal, Twilight Zone, Isaac Asimov's Science Fiction Magazine, Analog, Amazing,* and *Whispers,* as well as in such anthologies as *The Best of Shadows, The Year's Best Horror Stories, Great Ghost Stories,* and *Visions of Fantasy: Tales from the Masters.* He is the author of the horror novels *The Boy With Penny Eyes, Totentanz, Campbell Wood,* and *The Worms,* the science fiction novel *Moonbane,* the mystery novels *Cold Night* and *Summer Cool,* and has edited two volumes of humor, *The Fireside Treasury of Great Humor* and *The Fireside Treasury of New Humor.* He is the author of columns for the Horror Writers of America newsletter and *Mystery Scene* magazine. He lives in New York's Hudson Valley with his wife and two sons, and is currently at work on his next novel.

John Saul is "a writer with the touch for raising gooseflesh."
—*Detroit News*

John Saul has produced one bestseller after another: masterful tales of terror and psychological suspense. Each of his works is as shocking, as intense and as stunningly real as those that preceded it.

DON'T MISS
THESE CURRENT
Bantam Bestsellers

☐	28390	**THE AMATEUR** Robert Littell	$4.95
☐	28525	**THE DEBRIEFING** Robert Littell	$4.95
☐	28362	**COREY LANE** Norman Zollinger	$4.50
☐	27636	**PASSAGE TO QUIVIRA** Norman Zollinger	$4.50
☐	27759	**RIDER TO CIBOLA** Norman Zollinger	$3.95
☐	27811	**DOCTORS** Erich Segal	$5.95
☐	28179	**TREVAYNE** Robert Ludlum	$5.95
☐	27807	**PARTNERS** John Martel	$4.95
☐	28058	**EVA LUNA** Isabel Allende	$4.95
☐	27597	**THE BONFIRE OF THE VANITIES** Tom Wolfe	$5.95
☐	27510	**THE BUTCHER'S THEATER** Jonathan Kellerman	$4.95
☐	27800	**THE ICARUS AGENDA** Robert Ludlum	$5.95
☐	27891	**PEOPLE LIKE US** Dominick Dunne	$4.95
☐	27953	**TO BE THE BEST** Barbara Taylor Bradford	$5.95
☐	26892	**THE GREAT SANTINI** Pat Conroy	$5.95
☐	26574	**SACRED SINS** Nora Roberts	$3.95
☐	28436	**PAYMENT IN BLOOD** Elizabeth George	$4.95

Buy them at your local bookstore or use this page to order.

Bantam Books, Dept. FB, 414 East Golf Road, Des Plaines, IL 60016

Please send me the items I have checked above. I am enclosing $_____
(please add $2.00 to cover postage and handling). Send check or money
order, no cash or C.O.D.s please.

Mr/Ms _____

Address _____

City/State _____ Zip _____

FB–10/90

Please allow four to six weeks for delivery.
Prices and availability subject to change without notice.